Jimmy Gownley's

AMELIA RULES!™

Into Graceland

Atheneum Books for Young Readers
New York London Toronto Sydney

visit us at www.abdopublishing.com

Reinforced library bound edition published in 2013 by Spotlight, a division of the ABDO Group, PO Box 398166, Minneapolis, MN 55439. Spotlight produces high-quality reinforced library bound editions for schools and libraries. Published by agreement with Atheneum Books for Young Readers, an imprint of Simon & Schuster Children's Publishing Division.

Printed in the United States of America, North Mankato, Minnesota.
102012
012013
This book contains at least 10% recycled materials.

Book design by Sonia Chaghatzbanian

Library of Congress Cataloging-in-Publication Data

Gownley, Jimmy.
   Amelia in into Graceland / [Jimmy Gownley]. -- Reinforced library bound ed.
      p. cm. -- (Jimmy Gownley's Amelia rules!)
   Summary: When Amelia's mother inherits her aunt's house across town, Amelia imagines
her life changing in devastating ways, beginning with having to leave her group of
friends and join the ninjas.
   ISBN 978-1-61479-071-6
   [1. Graphic novels. 2. Moving, Household--Fiction. 3. Friendship--Fiction.] I. Title.
   PZ7.G69Amm 2013
   741.5'973--dc23
                                          2012026910

All Spotlight books are reinforced library bindings
and manufactured in the United States of America.

To Major Stephen M. Murphy.
This book is for you, with thanks
for your service to our country,
and for your friendship.

MEET THE GANG

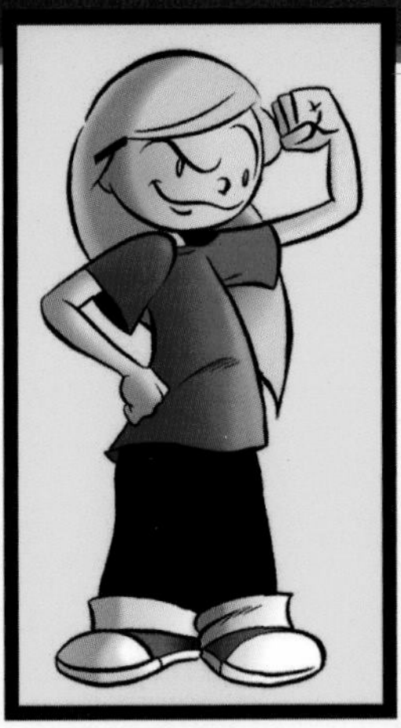

Amelia Louise McBride:
Our heroine. Wise cracking, yet sweet. She spends her time hanging out with friends and her aunt Tanner.

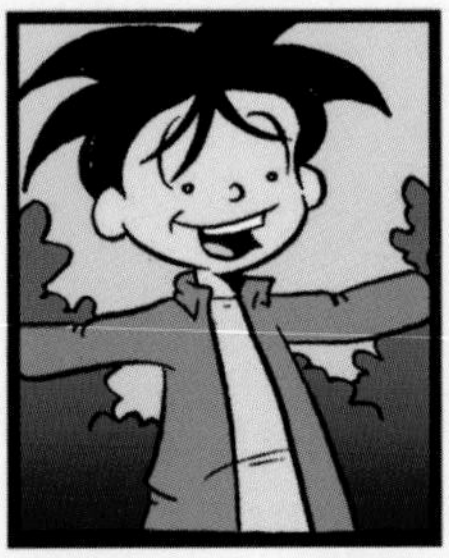

Reggie Grabinsky:
A.k.a. Captain Amazing. Founder of G.A.S.P., which he forces . . . er, encourages, his friends to join.

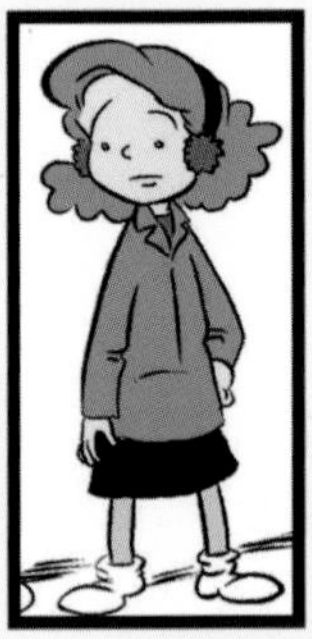

Rhonda Bleenie:
Smart, stubborn, and loud. She wears her heart on her sleeve and it's filled with love for Reggie.

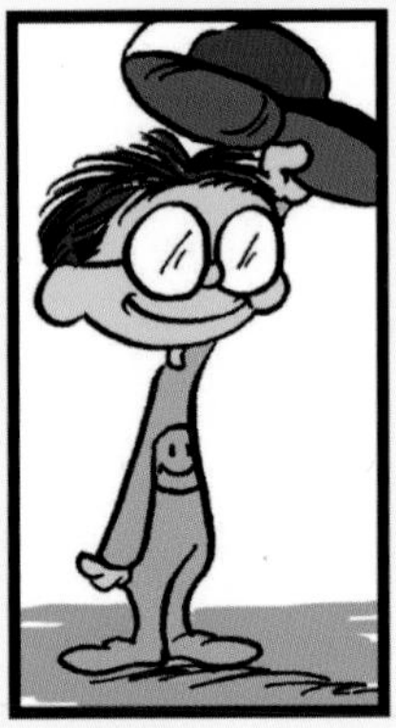

Pajamaman:
Never speaks. Always cool. His feetie jammies tell you what's on his mind.

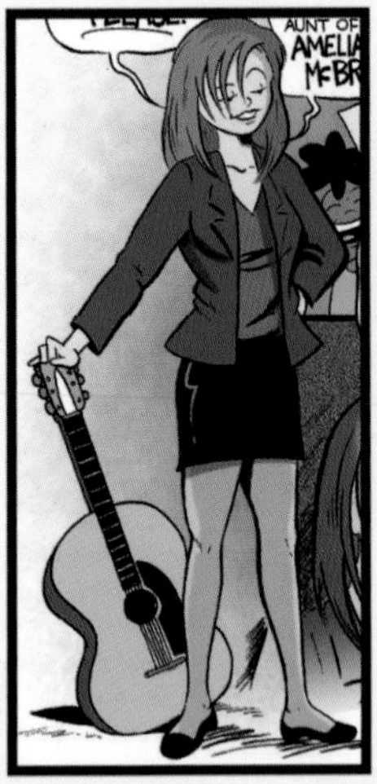
AUNT OF

Tanner:
Amelia's aunt and a former rock 'n' roll superstar.

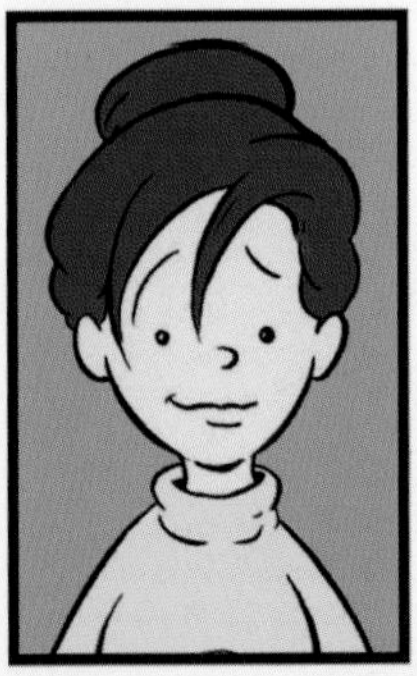

Amelia's Mom (Mary):
Starting a new life in Pennsylvania with Amelia after the divorce.

Amelia's Dad:
Still lives in New York, and misses Amelia terribly.

G.A.S.P.
Gathering Of Awesome Super Pals. The superhero club Reggie founded.

Park View Terrace Ninjas:
Club across town and nemesis to G.A.S.P.

Kyle:
The main ninja. Kind of a jerk but not without charm.

Joan:
Former Park View Terrace Ninja (nemesis of G.A.S.P.), now friends with Amelia and company.

Tweenie Zeenie:
A local kid-run magazine and Web site.

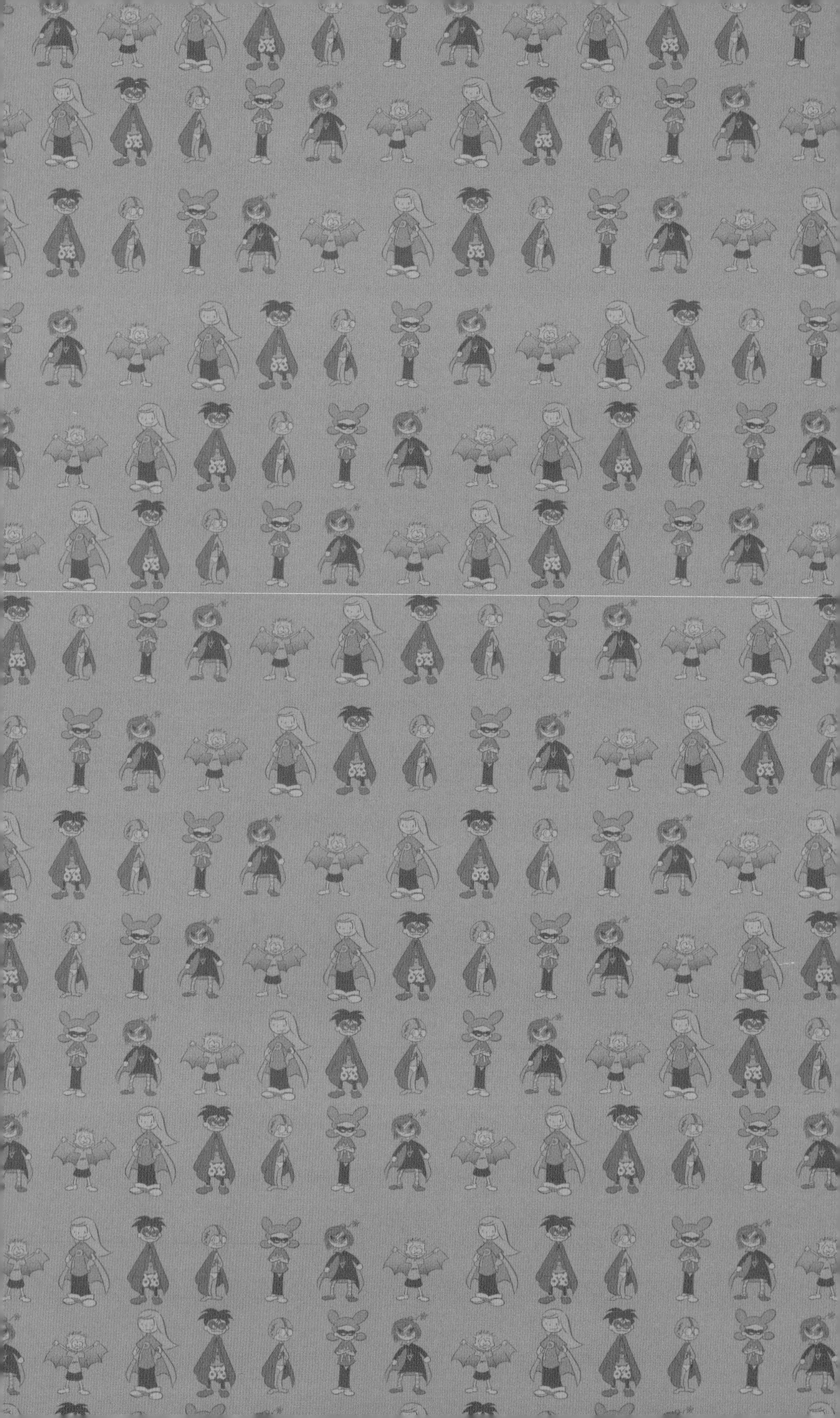

Into
Graceland

MOVING?

AT FIRST I JUST FIGURED I ***HEARD*** HER WRONG.

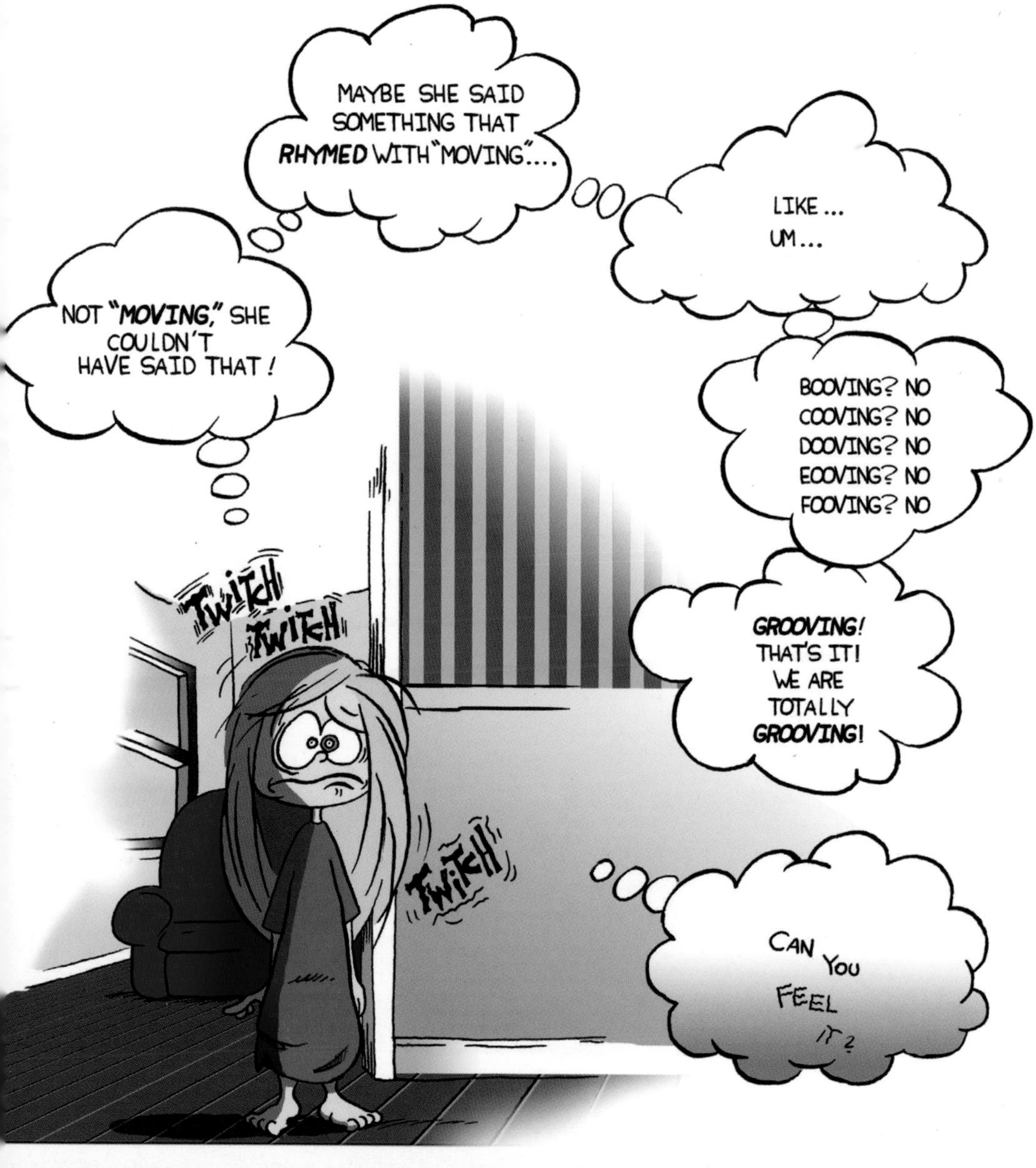
NOT "***MOVING,***" SHE COULDN'T HAVE SAID THAT!
MAYBE SHE SAID SOMETHING THAT ***RHYMED*** WITH "MOVING"....
LIKE... UM...
BOOVING? NO
COOVING? NO
DOOVING? NO
EOOVING? NO
FOOVING? NO
GROOVING! THAT'S IT! WE ARE TOTALLY ***GROOVING!***
CAN YOU FEEL IT?
TWITCH
TWITCH
TWITCH

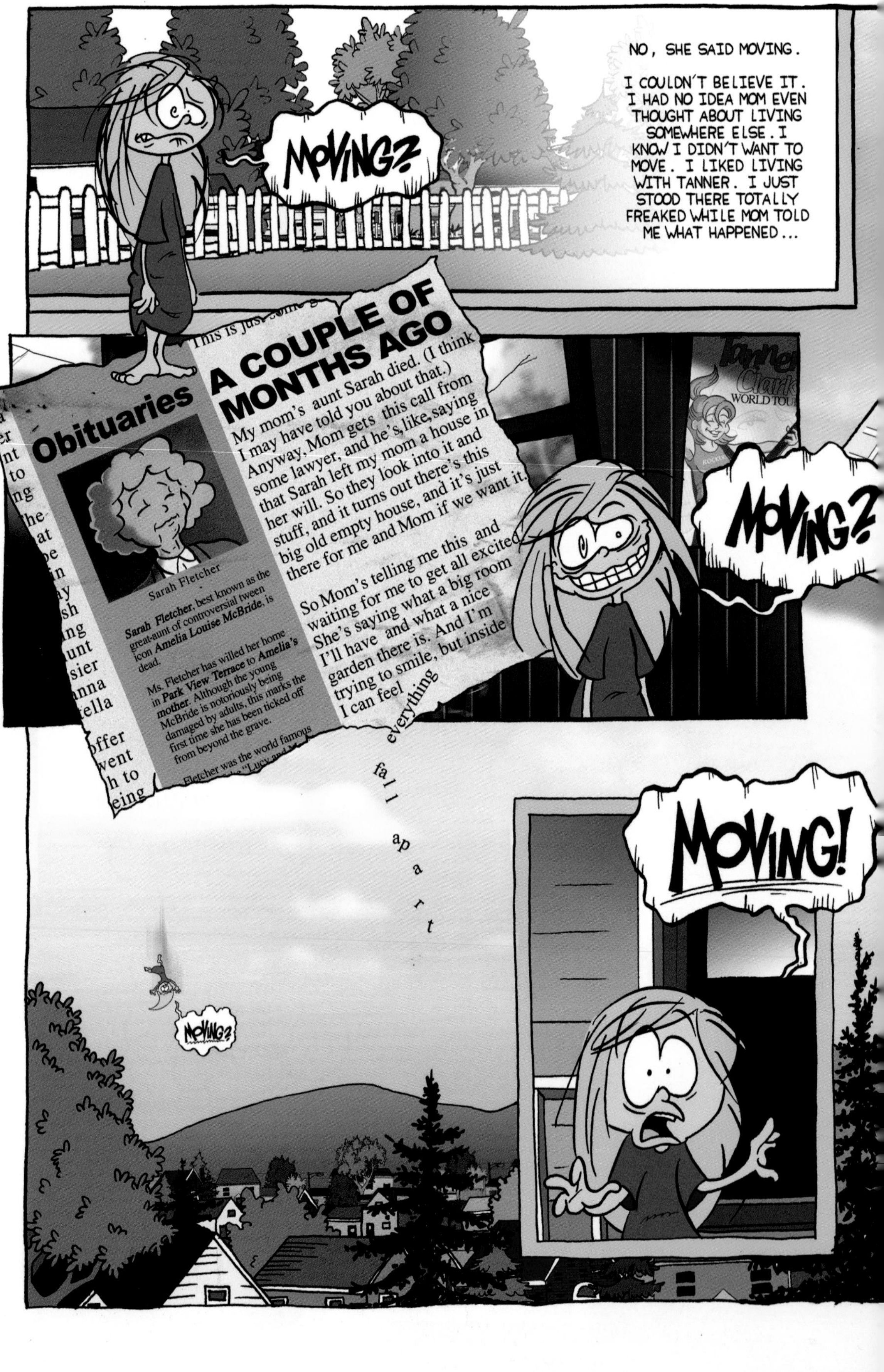
MOVING?
NO, SHE SAID MOVING.
I COULDN'T BELIEVE IT. I HAD NO IDEA MOM EVEN THOUGHT ABOUT LIVING SOMEWHERE ELSE. I KNOW I DIDN'T WANT TO MOVE. I LIKED LIVING WITH TANNER. I JUST STOOD THERE TOTALLY FREAKED WHILE MOM TOLD ME WHAT HAPPENED...
Obituaries
Sarah Fletcher
Sarah Fletcher, best known as the great-aunt of controversial tween icon Amelia Louise McBride, is dead.
Ms. Fletcher has willed her home in Park View Terrace to Amelia's mother. Although the young McBride is notoriously being damaged by adults, this marks the first time she has been ticked off from beyond the grave.
Fletcher was the world famous
A COUPLE OF MONTHS AGO
My mom's aunt Sarah died. (I think I may have told you about that.) Anyway, Mom gets this call from some lawyer, and he's, like, saying that Sarah left my mom a house in her will. So they look into it and stuff, and it turns out there's this big old empty house, and it's just there for me and Mom if we want it.
So Mom's telling me this and waiting for me to get all excited. She's saying what a big room I'll have and what a nice garden there is. And I'm trying to smile, but inside I can feel
everything
fall
apart
Tanner Clark WORLD TOUR
MOVING?
MOVING?
MOVING!

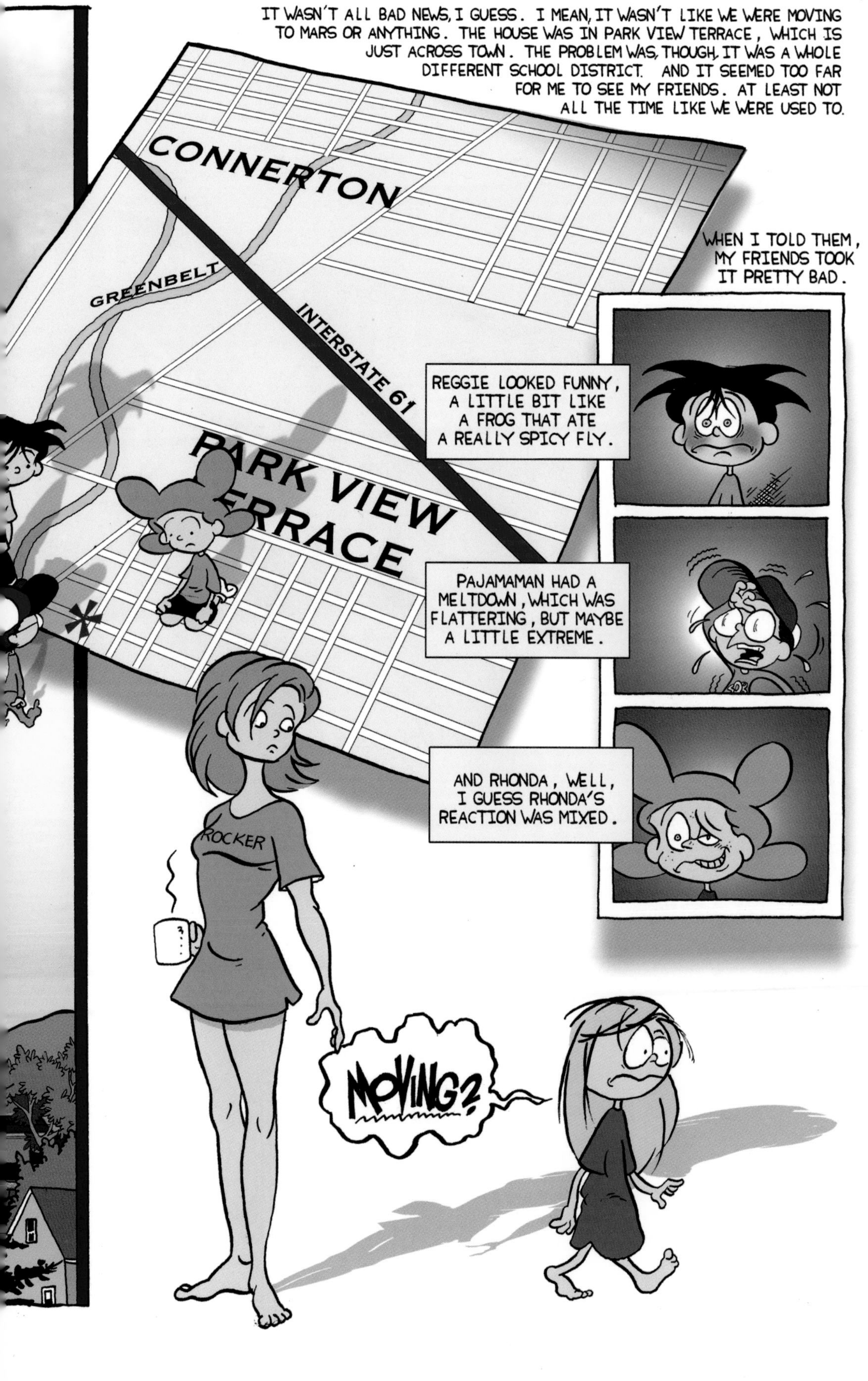
IT WASN'T ALL BAD NEWS, I GUESS. I MEAN, IT WASN'T LIKE WE WERE MOVING TO MARS OR ANYTHING. THE HOUSE WAS IN PARK VIEW TERRACE, WHICH IS JUST ACROSS TOWN. THE PROBLEM WAS, THOUGH, IT WAS A WHOLE DIFFERENT SCHOOL DISTRICT. AND IT SEEMED TOO FAR FOR ME TO SEE MY FRIENDS. AT LEAST NOT ALL THE TIME LIKE WE WERE USED TO.
CONNERTON
GREENBELT
INTERSTATE 61
PARK VIEW TERRACE
WHEN I TOLD THEM, MY FRIENDS TOOK IT PRETTY BAD.
REGGIE LOOKED FUNNY, A LITTLE BIT LIKE A FROG THAT ATE A REALLY SPICY FLY.
PAJAMAMAN HAD A MELTDOWN, WHICH WAS FLATTERING, BUT MAYBE A LITTLE EXTREME.
AND RHONDA, WELL, I GUESS RHONDA'S REACTION WAS MIXED.
ROCKER
MOVING?

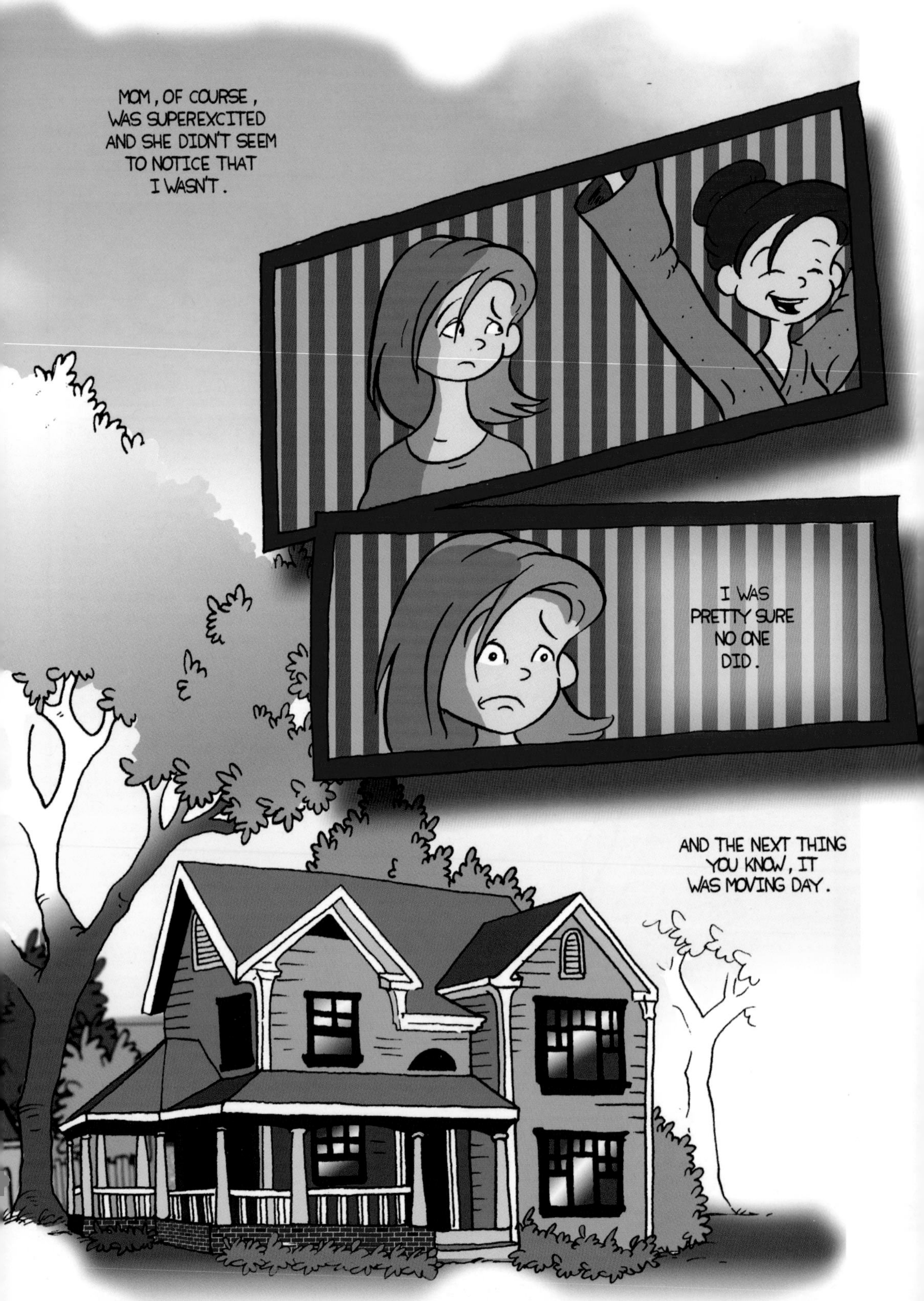
MOM, OF COURSE, WAS SUPEREXCITED AND SHE DIDN'T SEEM TO NOTICE THAT I WASN'T.
I WAS PRETTY SURE NO ONE DID.
AND THE NEXT THING YOU KNOW, IT WAS MOVING DAY.

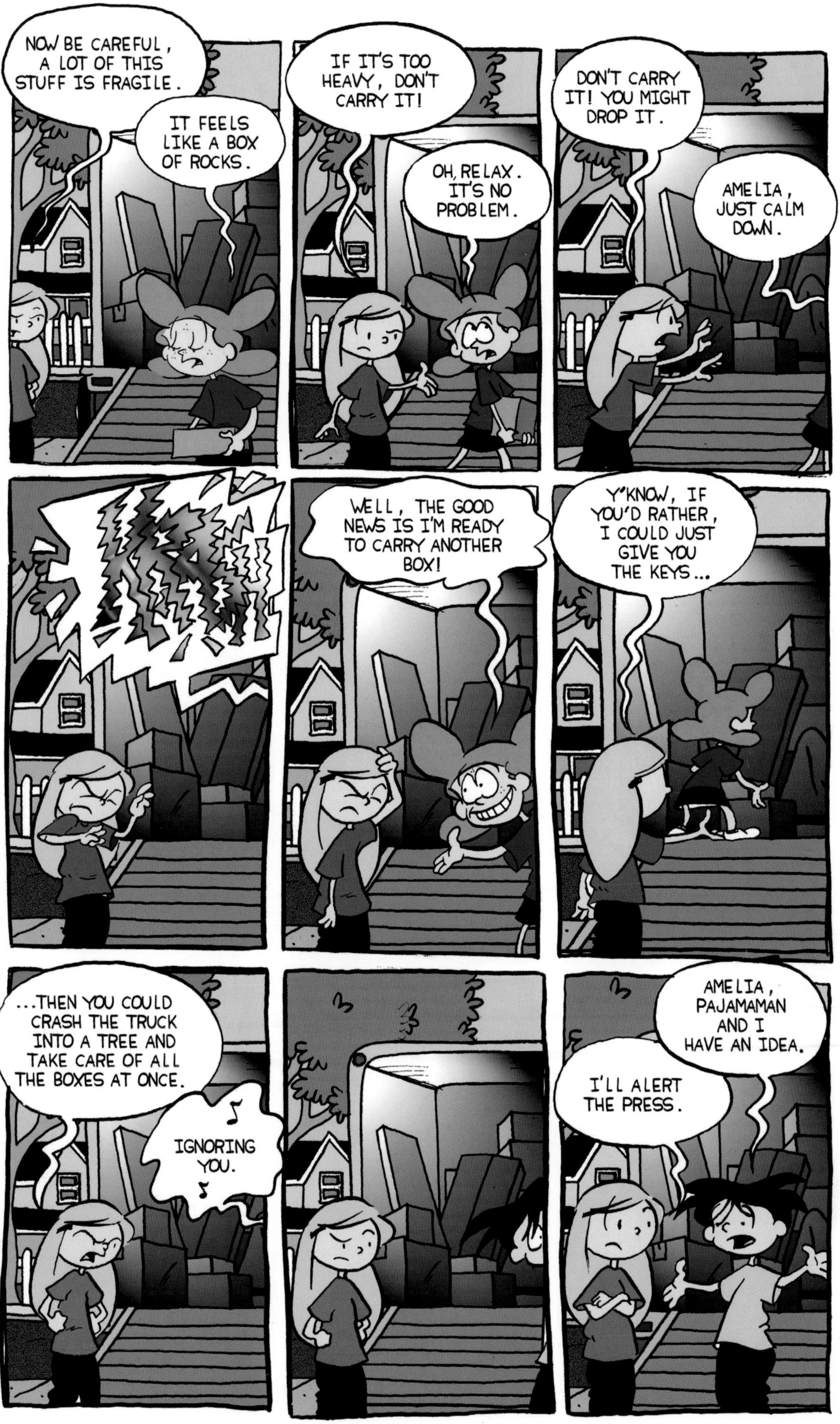
NOW BE CAREFUL, A LOT OF THIS STUFF IS FRAGILE.
IT FEELS LIKE A BOX OF ROCKS.
IF IT'S TOO HEAVY, DON'T CARRY IT!
OH, RELAX. IT'S NO PROBLEM.
DON'T CARRY IT! YOU MIGHT DROP IT.
AMELIA, JUST CALM DOWN.
WELL, THE GOOD NEWS IS I'M READY TO CARRY ANOTHER BOX!
Y'KNOW, IF YOU'D RATHER, I COULD JUST GIVE YOU THE KEYS...
...THEN YOU COULD CRASH THE TRUCK INTO A TREE AND TAKE CARE OF ALL THE BOXES AT ONCE.
IGNORING YOU.
AMELIA, PAJAMAMAN AND I HAVE AN IDEA.
I'LL ALERT THE PRESS.

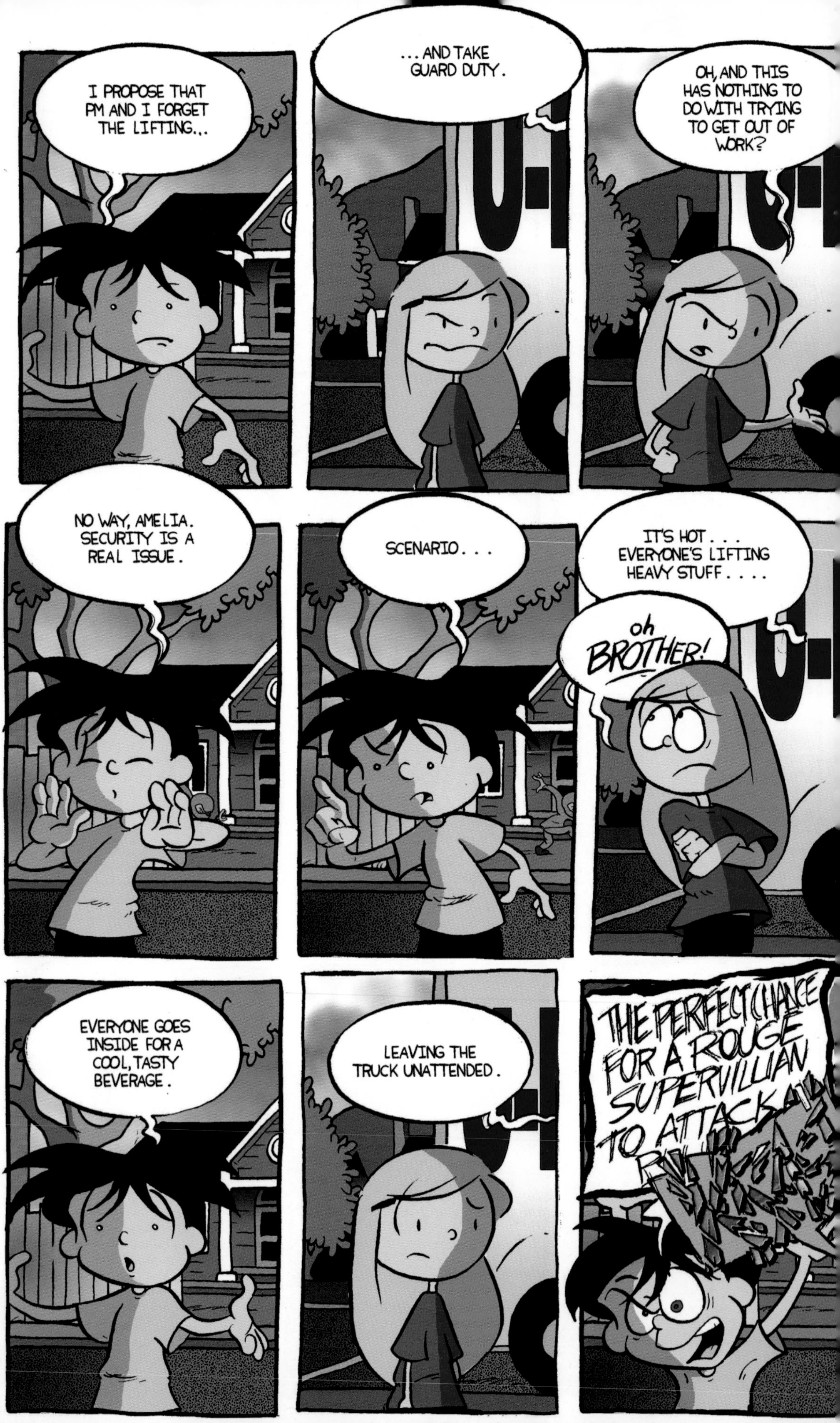
I PROPOSE THAT PM AND I FORGET THE LIFTING...
...AND TAKE GUARD DUTY.
OH, AND THIS HAS NOTHING TO DO WITH TRYING TO GET OUT OF WORK?
NO WAY, AMELIA. SECURITY IS A REAL ISSUE.
SCENARIO...
IT'S HOT... EVERYONE'S LIFTING HEAVY STUFF....
oh BROTHER!
EVERYONE GOES INSIDE FOR A COOL, TASTY BEVERAGE.
LEAVING THE TRUCK UNATTENDED.
THE PERFECT CHANCE FOR A ROUGE SUPERVILLIAN TO ATTACK

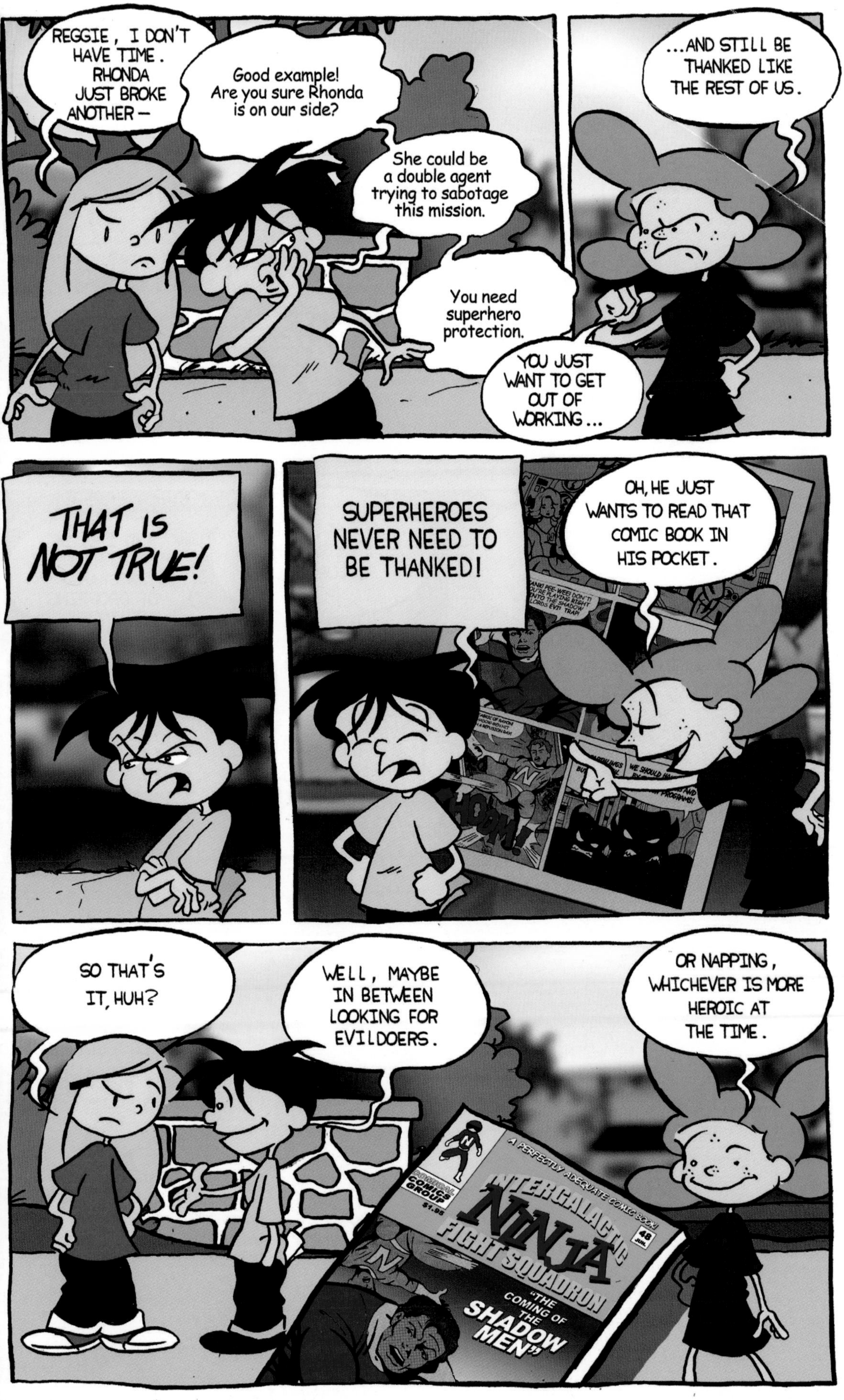
REGGIE, I DON'T HAVE TIME. RHONDA JUST BROKE ANOTHER –
Good example! Are you sure Rhonda is on our side?
She could be a double agent trying to sabotage this mission.
You need superhero protection.
YOU JUST WANT TO GET OUT OF WORKING...
...AND STILL BE THANKED LIKE THE REST OF US.
THAT IS NOT TRUE!
SUPERHEROES NEVER NEED TO BE THANKED!
OH, HE JUST WANTS TO READ THAT COMIC BOOK IN HIS POCKET.
SO THAT'S IT, HUH?
WELL, MAYBE IN BETWEEN LOOKING FOR EVILDOERS.
OR NAPPING, WHICHEVER IS MORE HEROIC AT THE TIME.
A PERFECTLY ADEQUATE COMIC BOOK!
INTERGALACTIC NINJA FIGHT SQUADRON
"THE COMING OF THE SHADOW MEN"
COMICS GROUP
$1.95
48
JUN.

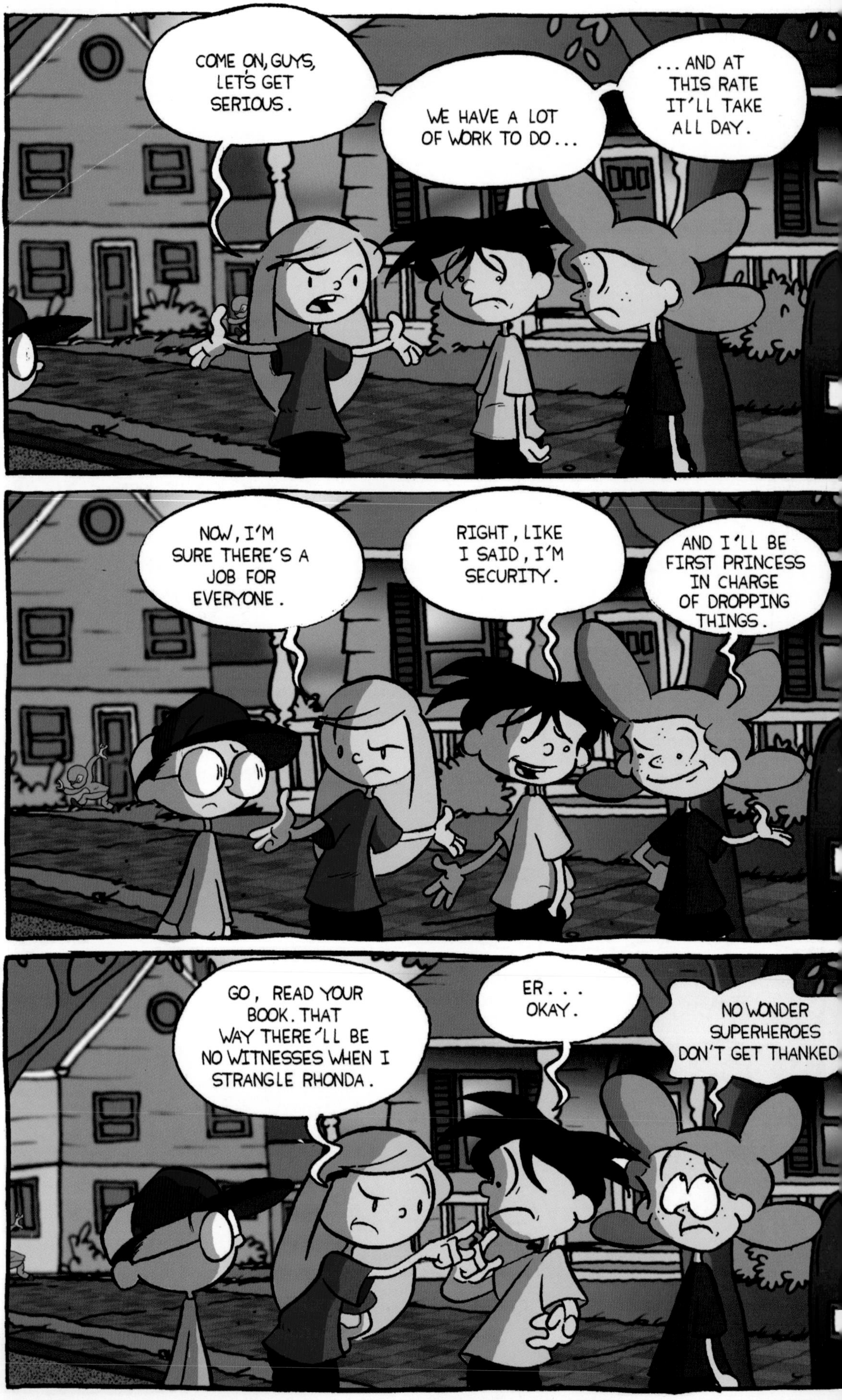
COME ON, GUYS, LET'S GET SERIOUS.
WE HAVE A LOT OF WORK TO DO...
...AND AT THIS RATE IT'LL TAKE ALL DAY.
NOW, I'M SURE THERE'S A JOB FOR EVERYONE.
RIGHT, LIKE I SAID, I'M SECURITY.
AND I'LL BE FIRST PRINCESS IN CHARGE OF DROPPING THINGS.
GO, READ YOUR BOOK. THAT WAY THERE'LL BE NO WITNESSES WHEN I STRANGLE RHONDA.
ER... OKAY.
NO WONDER SUPERHEROES DON'T GET THANKED

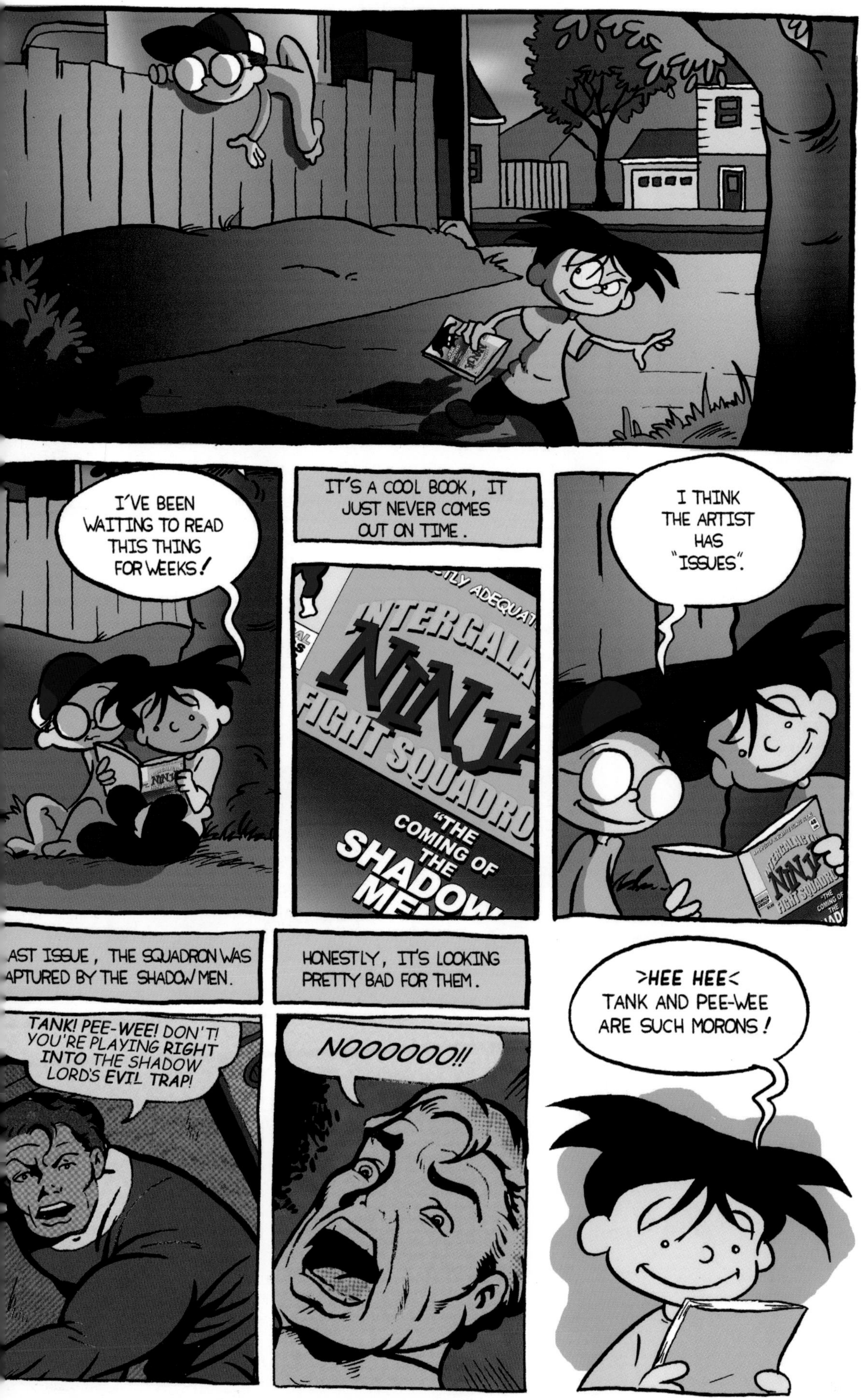
I'VE BEEN WAITING TO READ THIS THING FOR WEEKS!
IT'S A COOL BOOK, IT JUST NEVER COMES OUT ON TIME.
INTERGALA NINJA FIGHT SQUADRO "THE COMING OF THE SHADOW MEN
I THINK THE ARTIST HAS "ISSUES".
AST ISSUE, THE SQUADRON WAS APTURED BY THE SHADOW MEN.
HONESTLY, IT'S LOOKING PRETTY BAD FOR THEM.
TANK! PEE-WEE! DON'T! YOU'RE PLAYING RIGHT INTO THE SHADOW LORD'S EVIL TRAP!
NOOOOOO!!
>HEE HEE< TANK AND PEE-WEE ARE SUCH MORONS!

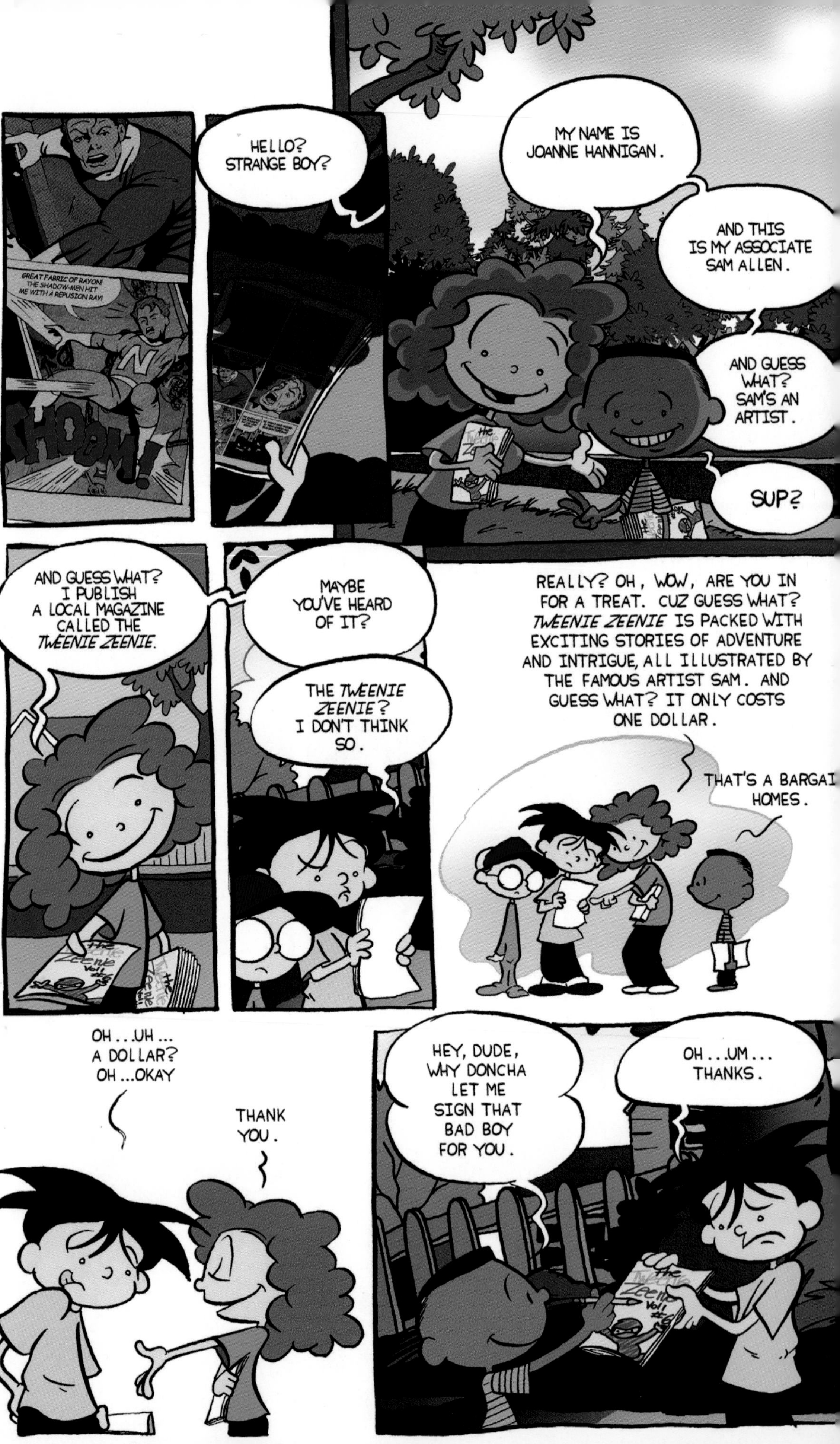
GREAT FABRIC OF RAYON! THE SHADOW-MEN HIT ME WITH A REPUSION RAY!
KHOOM!
HELLO? STRANGE BOY?
MY NAME IS JOANNE HANNIGAN.
AND THIS IS MY ASSOCIATE SAM ALLEN.
AND GUESS WHAT? SAM'S AN ARTIST.
SUP?
AND GUESS WHAT? I PUBLISH A LOCAL MAGAZINE CALLED THE *TWEENIE ZEENIE*.
MAYBE YOU'VE HEARD OF IT?
THE *TWEENIE ZEENIE*? I DON'T THINK SO.
REALLY? OH, WOW, ARE YOU IN FOR A TREAT. CUZ GUESS WHAT? *TWEENIE ZEENIE* IS PACKED WITH EXCITING STORIES OF ADVENTURE AND INTRIGUE, ALL ILLUSTRATED BY THE FAMOUS ARTIST SAM. AND GUESS WHAT? IT ONLY COSTS ONE DOLLAR.
THAT'S A BARGAI
HOMES.
OH...UH... A DOLLAR? OH...OKAY
THANK YOU.
HEY, DUDE, WHY DONCHA LET ME SIGN THAT BAD BOY FOR YOU.
OH...UM... THANKS.

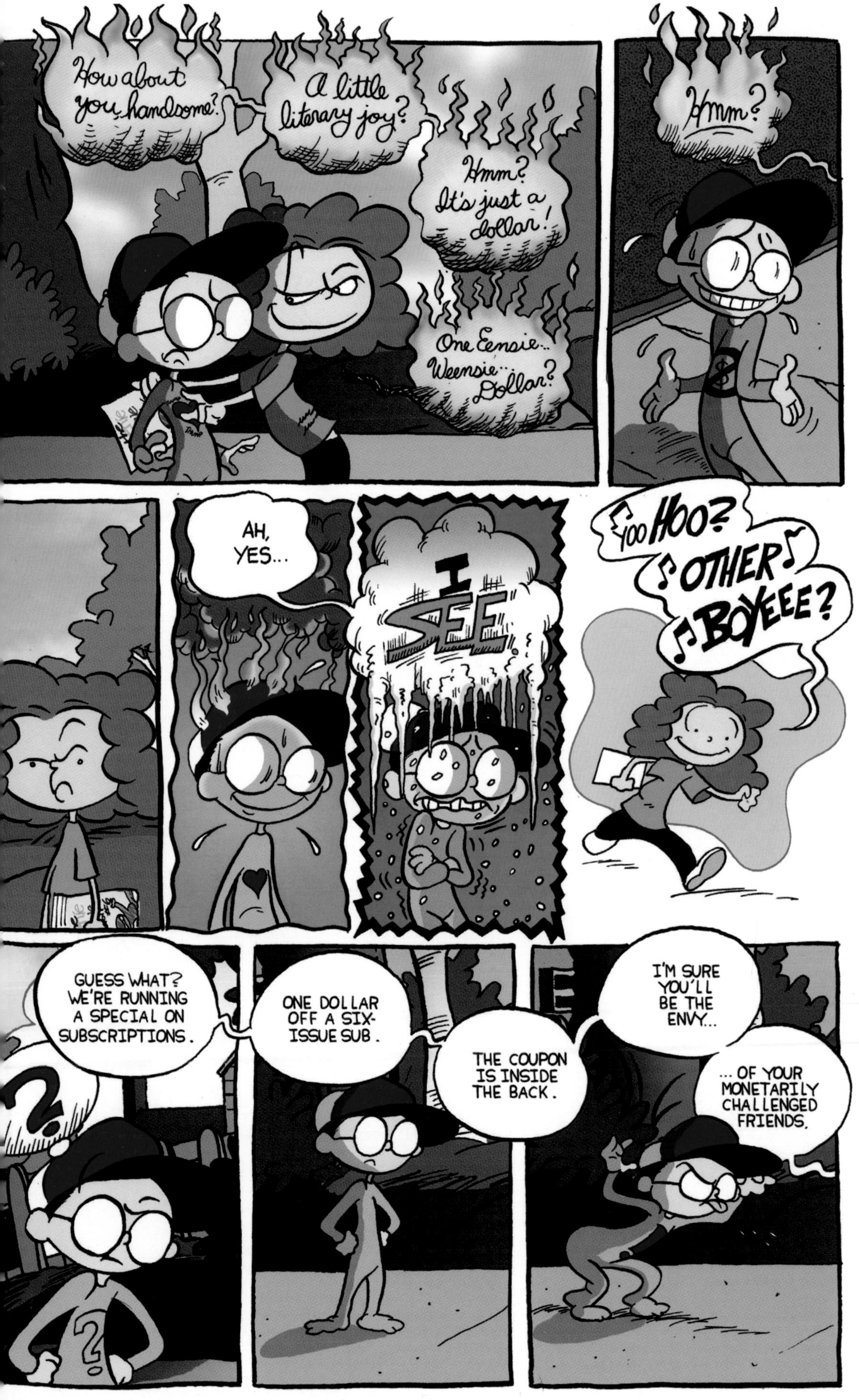
How about you, handsome?
A little literary joy?
Hmm? It's just a dollar!
One Eensie... Weensie... Dollar?
Hmm?
AH, YES...
I SEE
YOO HOO? OTHER BOYEEE?
GUESS WHAT? WE'RE RUNNING A SPECIAL ON SUBSCRIPTIONS.
ONE DOLLAR OFF A SIX-ISSUE SUB.
THE COUPON IS INSIDE THE BACK.
I'M SURE YOU'LL BE THE ENVY...
...OF YOUR MONETARILY CHALLENGED FRIENDS.

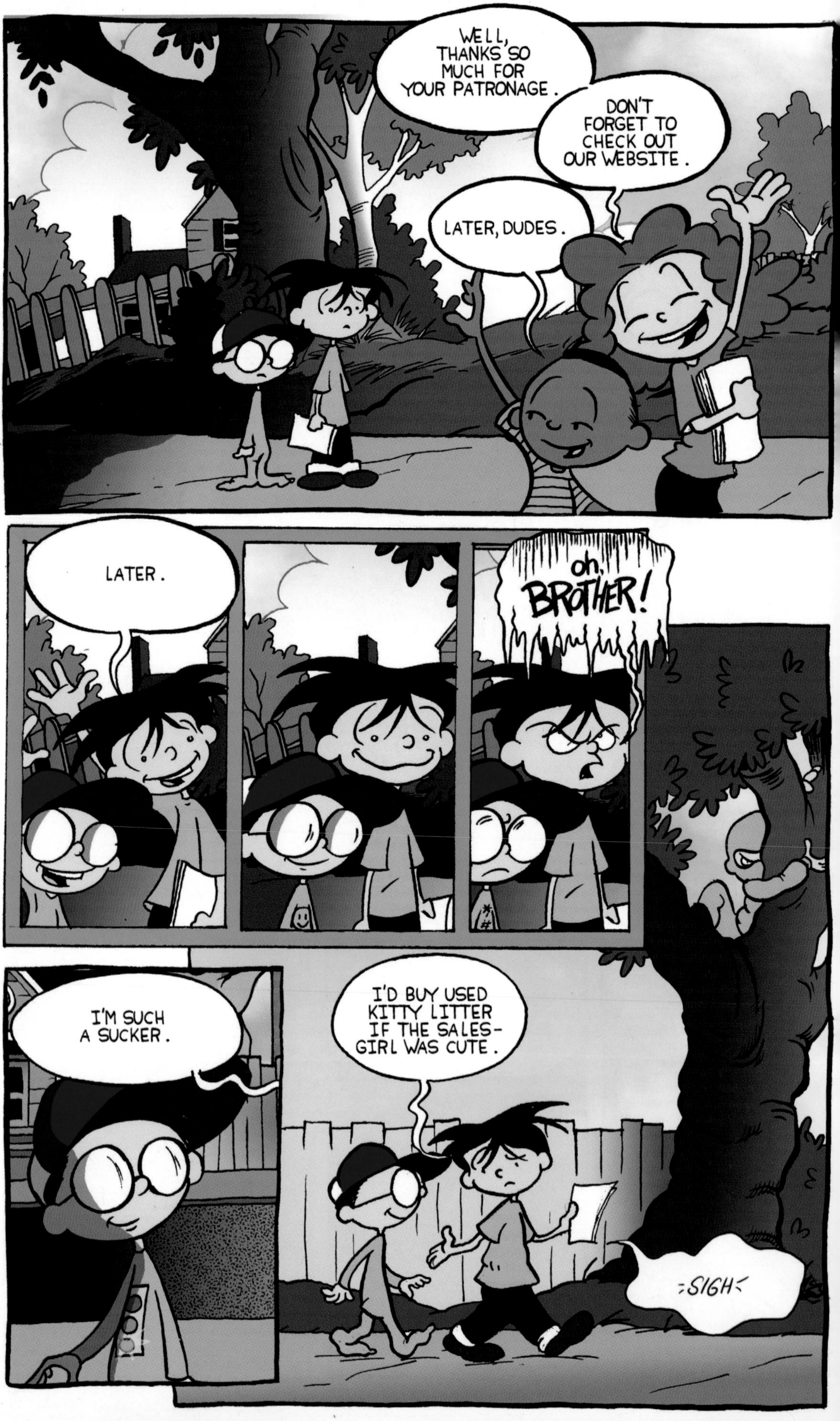
WELL, THANKS SO MUCH FOR YOUR PATRONAGE.
DON'T FORGET TO CHECK OUT OUR WEBSITE.
LATER, DUDES.
LATER.
oh, BROTHER!
I'M SUCH A SUCKER.
I'D BUY USED KITTY LITTER IF THE SALES-GIRL WAS CUTE.
SIGH

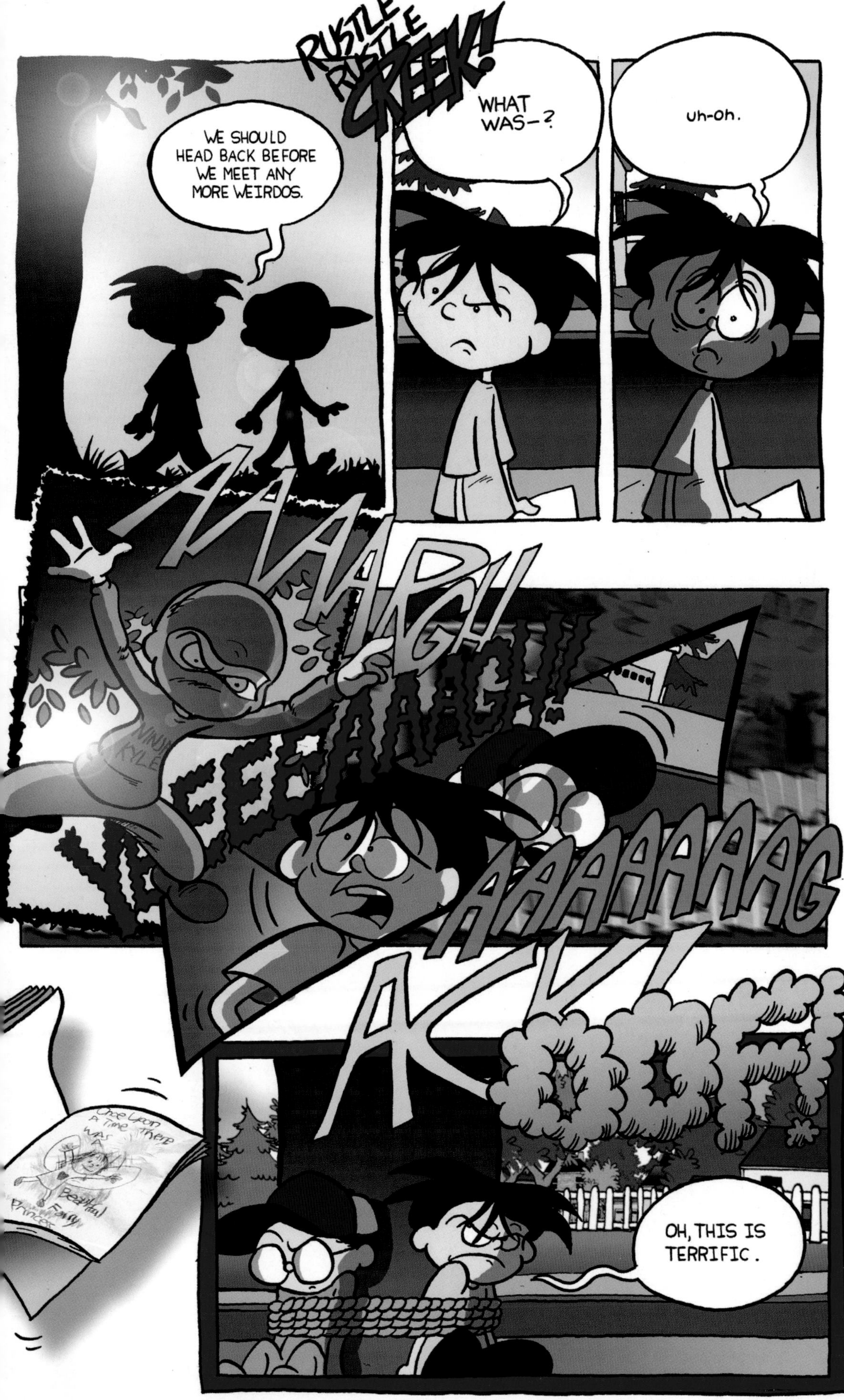
WE SHOULD HEAD BACK BEFORE WE MEET ANY MORE WEIRDOS.
RUSTLE RUSTLE CREEK!
WHAT WAS-?
uh-oh.
AAAAAGH!
YEEEAAAGH!
AAAAAAAAG
AK!
OOF!
NINJA KYLE
Once Upon A Time There Was A Beautiful Fairy Princess
OH, THIS IS TERRIFIC.

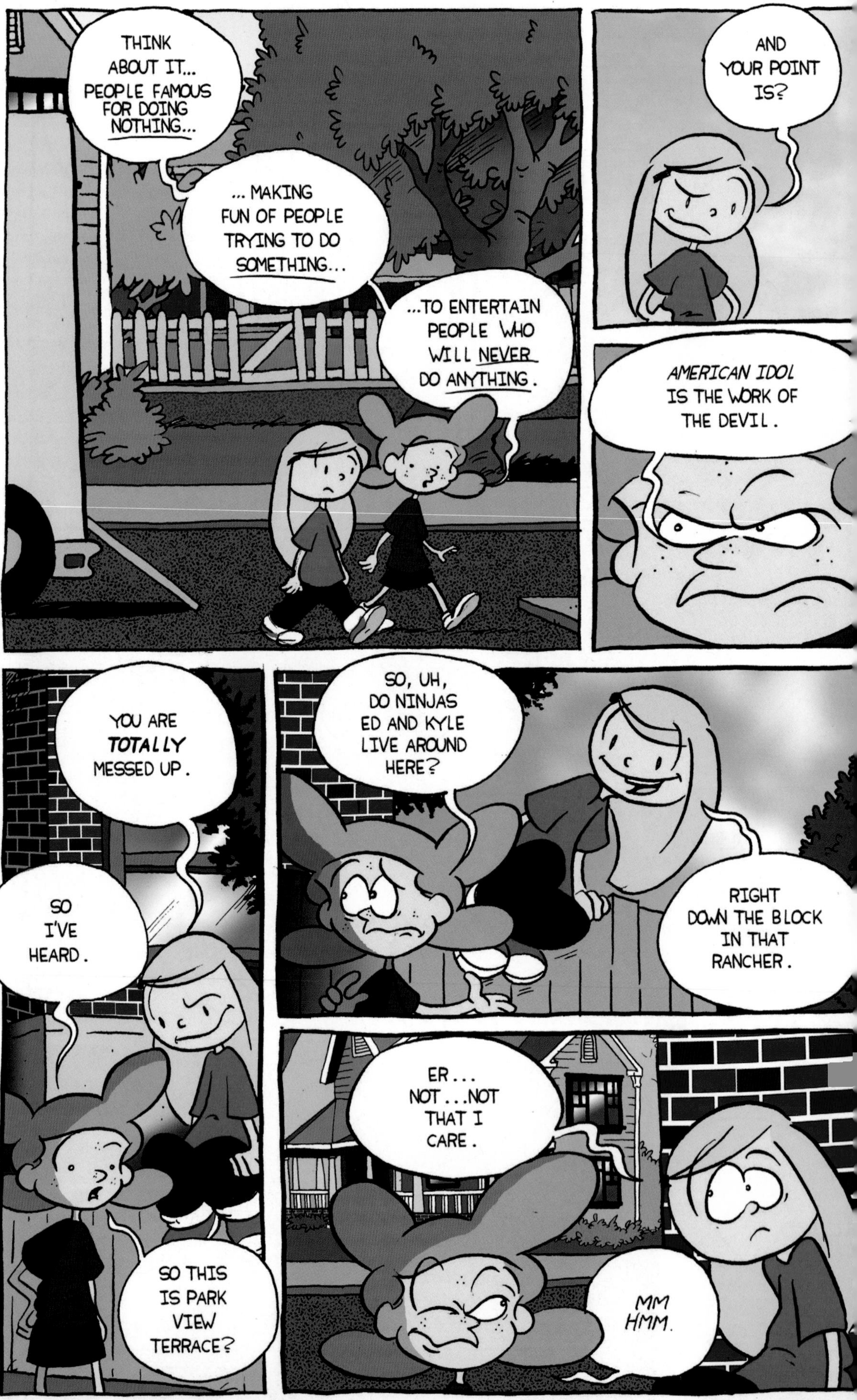

THINK ABOUT IT... PEOPLE FAMOUS FOR DOING NOTHING...
... MAKING FUN OF PEOPLE TRYING TO DO SOMETHING...
...TO ENTERTAIN PEOPLE WHO WILL NEVER DO ANYTHING.
AND YOUR POINT IS?
AMERICAN IDOL IS THE WORK OF THE DEVIL.
YOU ARE TOTALLY MESSED UP.
SO I'VE HEARD.
SO THIS IS PARK VIEW TERRACE?
SO, UH, DO NINJAS ED AND KYLE LIVE AROUND HERE?
RIGHT DOWN THE BLOCK IN THAT RANCHER.
ER... NOT...NOT THAT I CARE.
MM HMM.

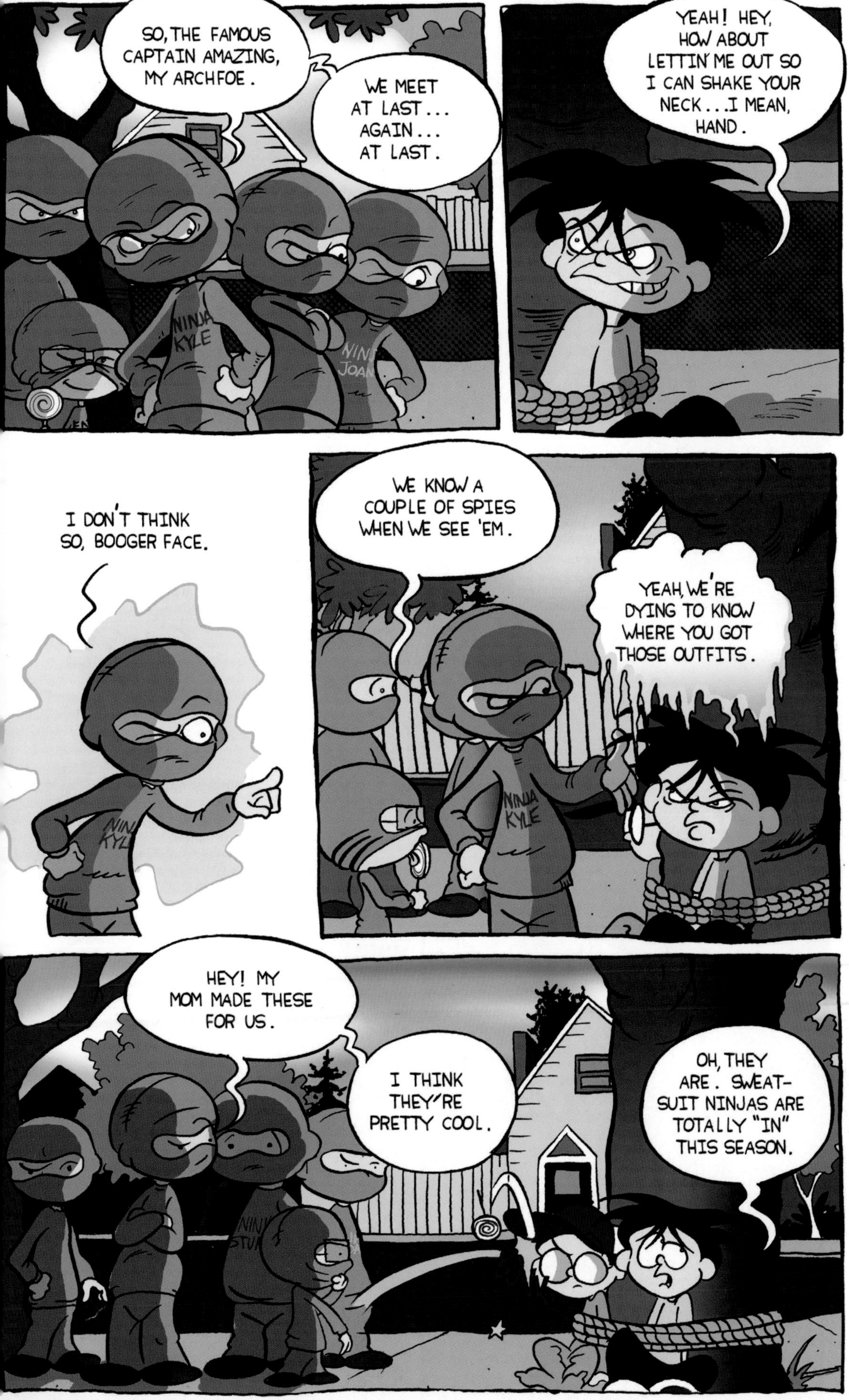
SO, THE FAMOUS CAPTAIN AMAZING, MY ARCHFOE.
WE MEET AT LAST... AGAIN... AT LAST.
NINJA KYLE
NINJ JOAN
YEAH! HEY, HOW ABOUT LETTIN' ME OUT SO I CAN SHAKE YOUR NECK...I MEAN, HAND.
I DON'T THINK SO, BOOGER FACE.
NINJ KYLE
WE KNOW A COUPLE OF SPIES WHEN WE SEE 'EM.
YEAH, WE'RE DYING TO KNOW WHERE YOU GOT THOSE OUTFITS.
NINJA KYLE
HEY! MY MOM MADE THESE FOR US.
I THINK THEY'RE PRETTY COOL.
OH, THEY ARE. SWEAT-SUIT NINJAS ARE TOTALLY "IN" THIS SEASON.

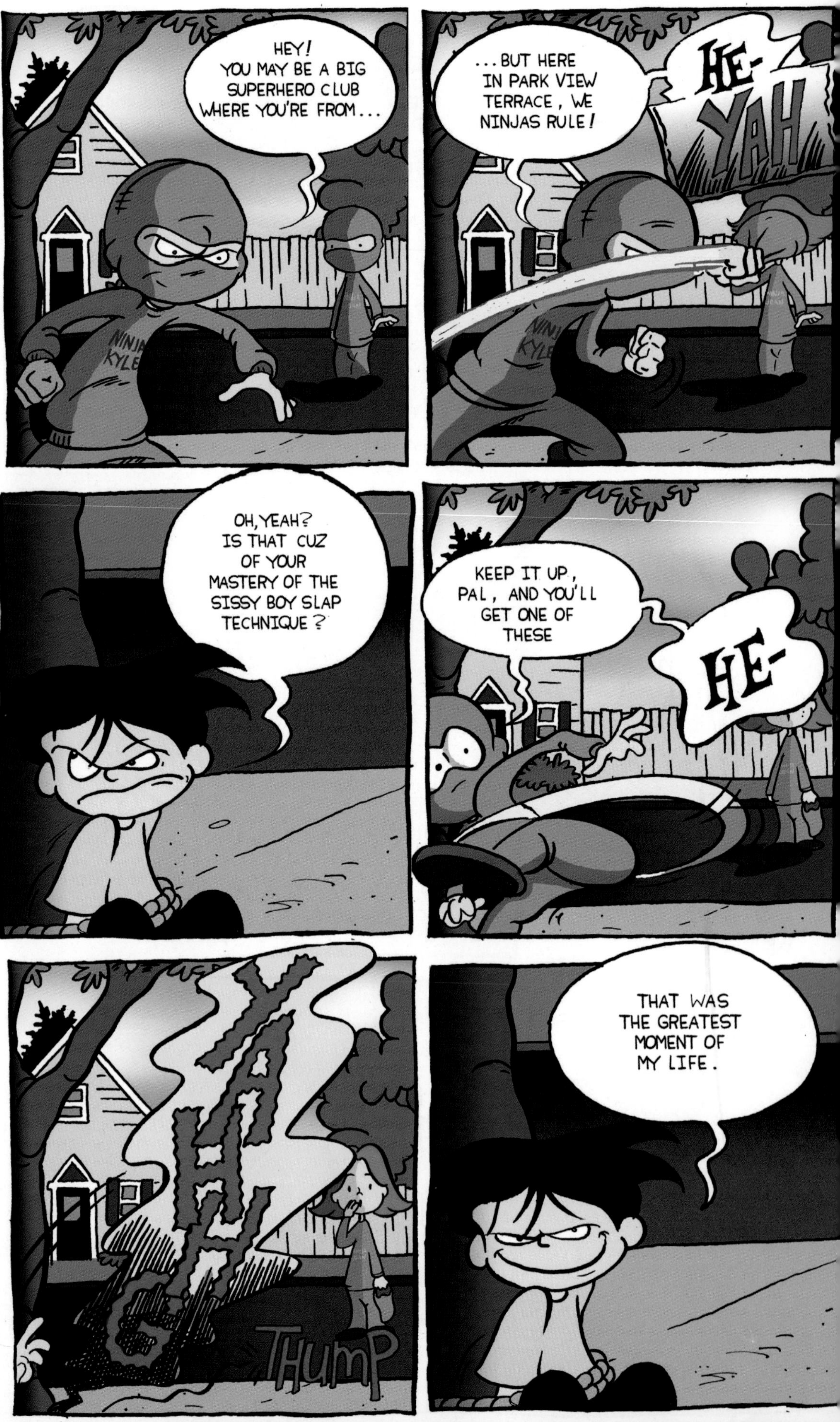
HEY! YOU MAY BE A BIG SUPERHERO CLUB WHERE YOU'RE FROM...
...BUT HERE IN PARK VIEW TERRACE, WE NINJAS RULE!
HE-YAH
NINJA KYLE
OH, YEAH? IS THAT CUZ OF YOUR MASTERY OF THE SISSY BOY SLAP TECHNIQUE?
KEEP IT UP, PAL, AND YOU'LL GET ONE OF THESE
HE-
YAHHH
THUMP
THAT WAS THE GREATEST MOMENT OF MY LIFE.

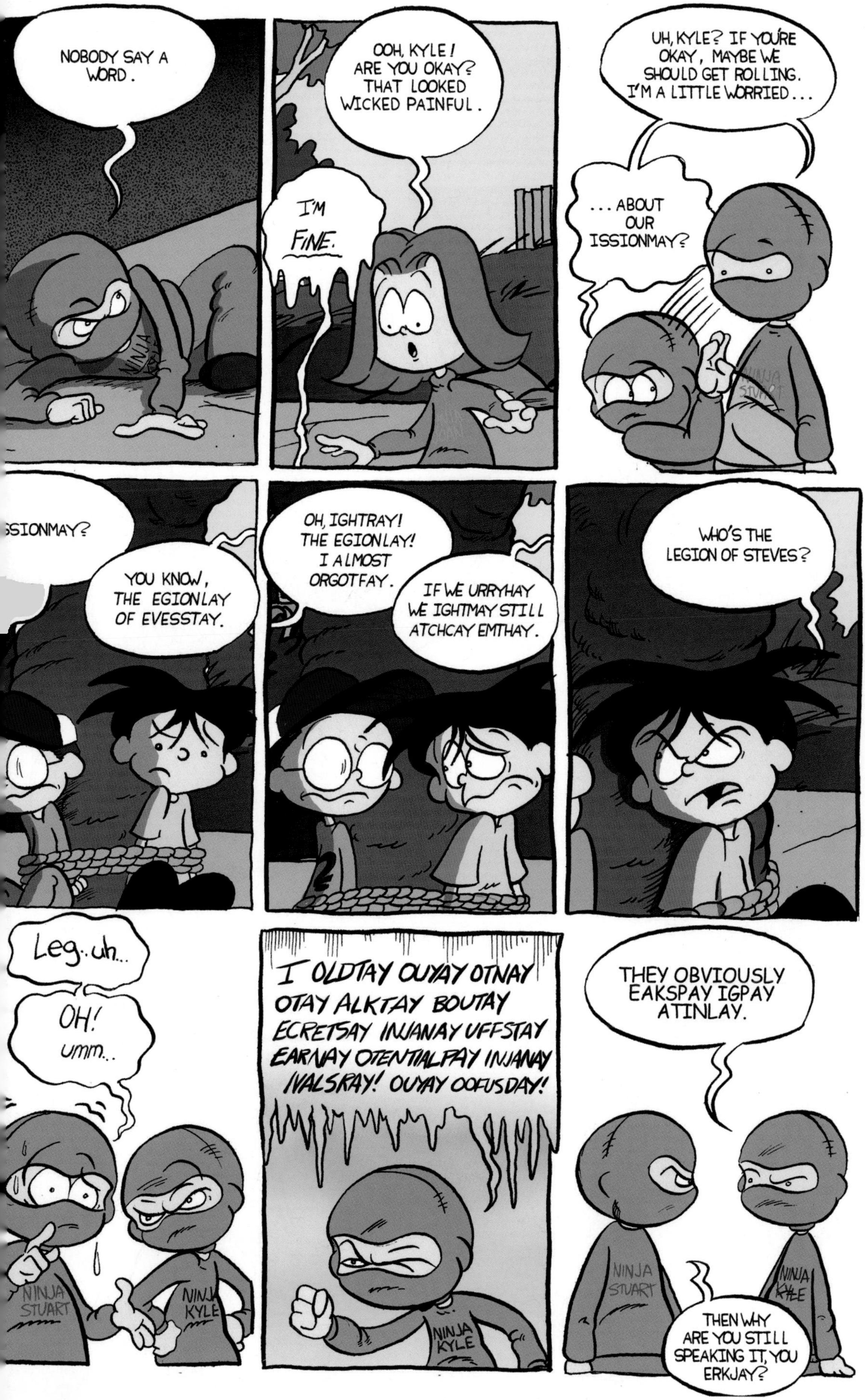
NOBODY SAY A WORD.
OOH, KYLE! ARE YOU OKAY? THAT LOOKED WICKED PAINFUL.
I'M FINE.
NINJA KYLE
UH, KYLE? IF YOU'RE OKAY, MAYBE WE SHOULD GET ROLLING. I'M A LITTLE WORRIED...
... ABOUT OUR ISSIONMAY?
SSIONMAY?
YOU KNOW, THE EGIONLAY OF EVESSTAY.
OH, IGHTRAY! THE EGIONLAY! I ALMOST ORGOTFAY.
IF WE URRYHAY WE IGHTMAY STILL ATCHCAY EMTHAY.
WHO'S THE LEGION OF STEVES?
Leg..uh...
OH! umm...
NINJA STUART
NINJA KYLE
I OLDTAY OUYAY OTNAY OTAY ALKTAY BOUTAY ECRETSAY INJANAY UFFSTAY EARNAY OTENTIALPAY INJANAY IVALSRAY! OUYAY OOFUSDAY!
NINJA KYLE
THEY OBVIOUSLY EAKSPAY IGPAY ATINLAY.
NINJA STUART
NINJA KYLE
THEN WHY ARE YOU STILL SPEAKING IT, YOU ERKJAY?

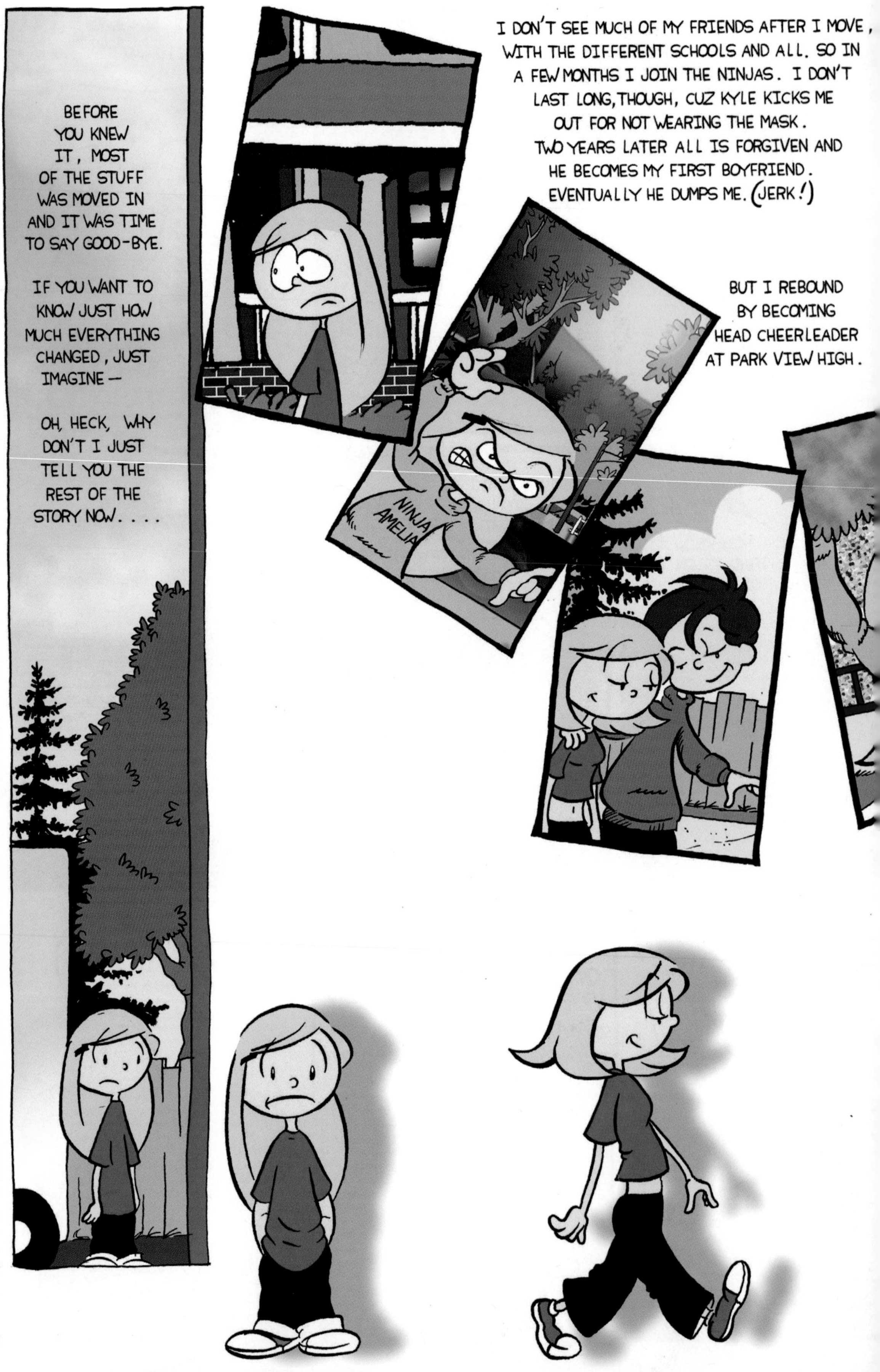
BEFORE YOU KNEW IT, MOST OF THE STUFF WAS MOVED IN AND IT WAS TIME TO SAY GOOD-BYE.
IF YOU WANT TO KNOW JUST HOW MUCH EVERYTHING CHANGED, JUST IMAGINE—
OH, HECK, WHY DON'T I JUST TELL YOU THE REST OF THE STORY NOW. . . .
I DON'T SEE MUCH OF MY FRIENDS AFTER I MOVE, WITH THE DIFFERENT SCHOOLS AND ALL. SO IN A FEW MONTHS I JOIN THE NINJAS. I DON'T LAST LONG, THOUGH, CUZ KYLE KICKS ME OUT FOR NOT WEARING THE MASK. TWO YEARS LATER ALL IS FORGIVEN AND HE BECOMES MY FIRST BOYFRIEND. EVENTUALLY HE DUMPS ME. (JERK!)
NINJA AMELIA
BUT I REBOUND BY BECOMING HEAD CHEERLEADER AT PARK VIEW HIGH.

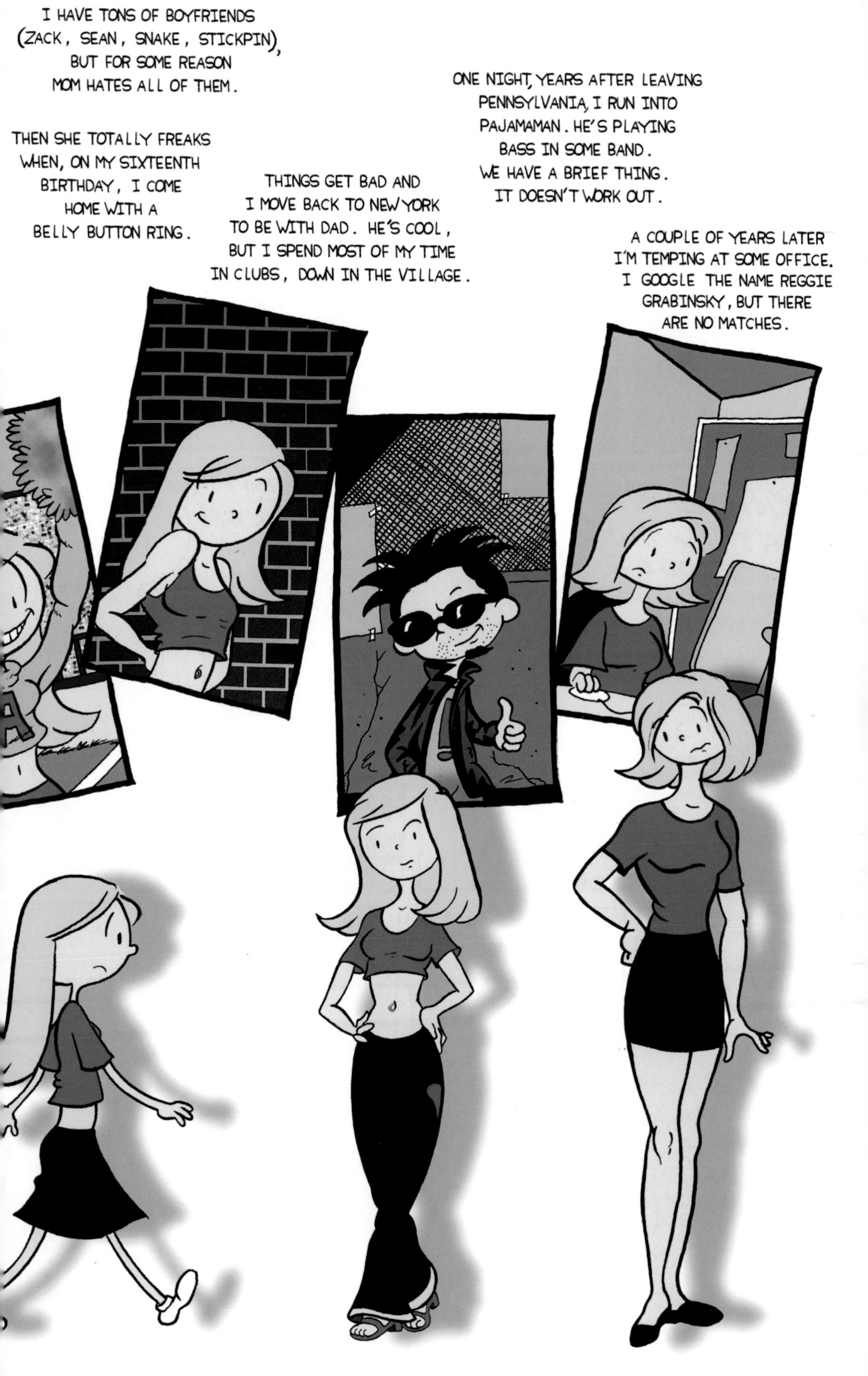
I HAVE TONS OF BOYFRIENDS (ZACK, SEAN, SNAKE, STICKPIN), BUT FOR SOME REASON MOM HATES ALL OF THEM.
THEN SHE TOTALLY FREAKS WHEN, ON MY SIXTEENTH BIRTHDAY, I COME HOME WITH A BELLY BUTTON RING.
THINGS GET BAD AND I MOVE BACK TO NEW YORK TO BE WITH DAD. HE'S COOL, BUT I SPEND MOST OF MY TIME IN CLUBS, DOWN IN THE VILLAGE.
ONE NIGHT, YEARS AFTER LEAVING PENNSYLVANIA, I RUN INTO PAJAMAMAN. HE'S PLAYING BASS IN SOME BAND. WE HAVE A BRIEF THING. IT DOESN'T WORK OUT.
A COUPLE OF YEARS LATER I'M TEMPING AT SOME OFFICE. I GOOGLE THE NAME REGGIE GRABINSKY, BUT THERE ARE NO MATCHES.

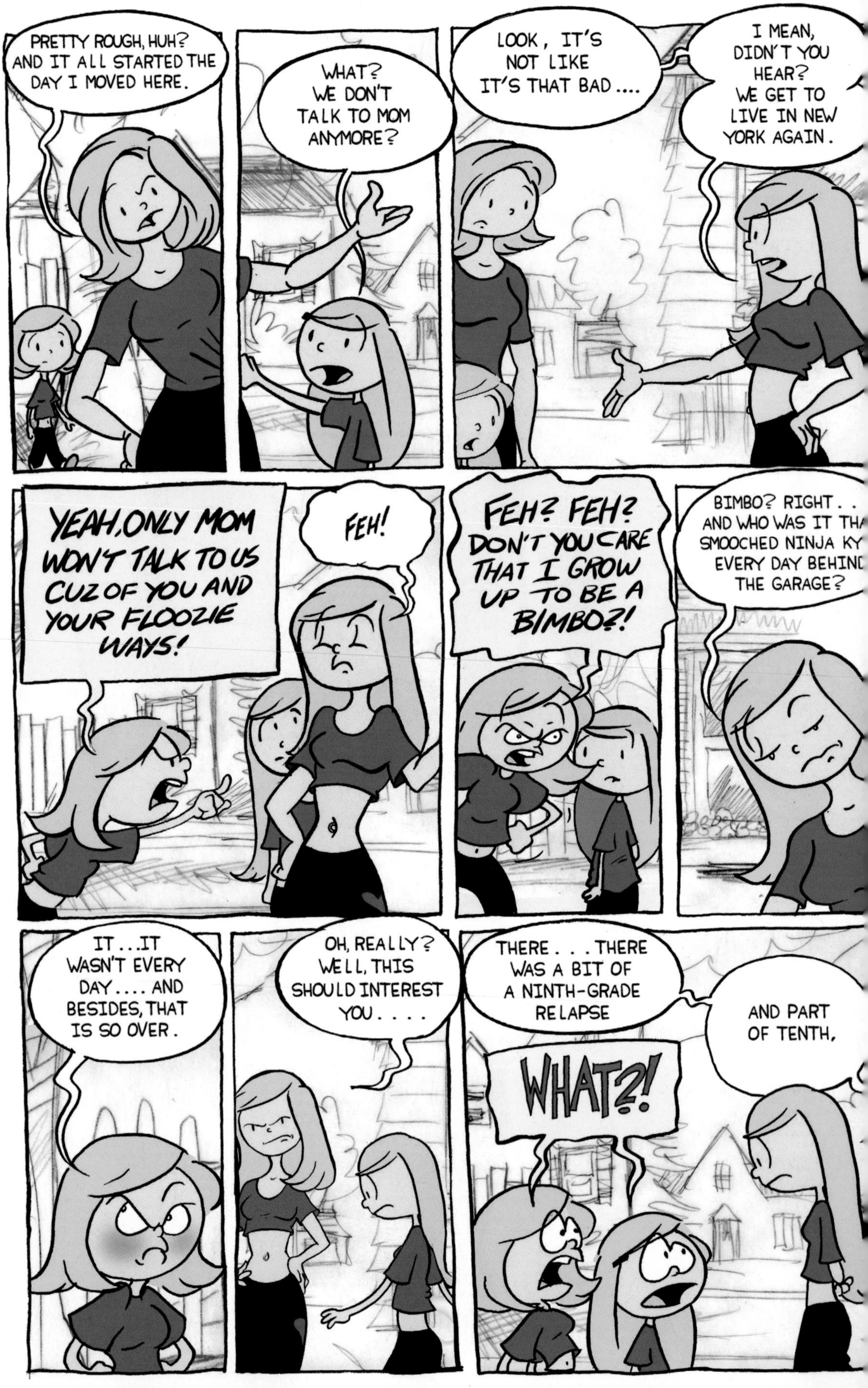
PRETTY ROUGH, HUH? AND IT ALL STARTED THE DAY I MOVED HERE.
WHAT? WE DON'T TALK TO MOM ANYMORE?
LOOK, IT'S NOT LIKE IT'S THAT BAD....
I MEAN, DIDN'T YOU HEAR? WE GET TO LIVE IN NEW YORK AGAIN.
YEAH, ONLY MOM WON'T TALK TO US CUZ OF YOU AND YOUR FLOOZIE WAYS!
FEH!
FEH? FEH? DON'T YOU CARE THAT I GROW UP TO BE A BIMBO?!
IT...IT WASN'T EVERY DAY.... AND BESIDES, THAT IS SO OVER.
OH, REALLY? WELL, THIS SHOULD INTEREST YOU....
THERE...THERE WAS A BIT OF A NINTH-GRADE RELAPSE
AND PART OF TENTH.
WHAT?!

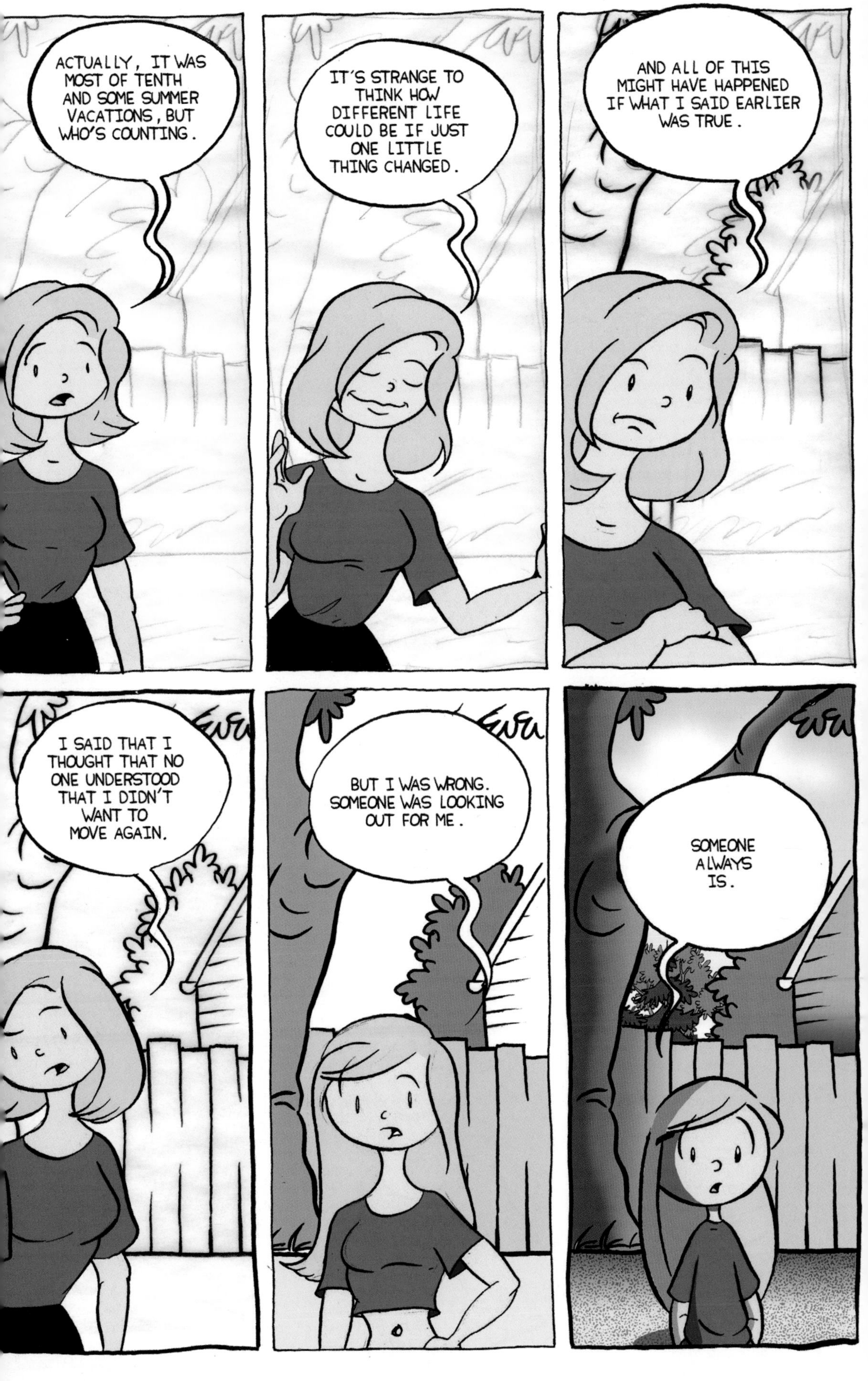
ACTUALLY, IT WAS MOST OF TENTH AND SOME SUMMER VACATIONS, BUT WHO'S COUNTING.
IT'S STRANGE TO THINK HOW DIFFERENT LIFE COULD BE IF JUST ONE LITTLE THING CHANGED.
AND ALL OF THIS MIGHT HAVE HAPPENED IF WHAT I SAID EARLIER WAS TRUE.
I SAID THAT I THOUGHT THAT NO ONE UNDERSTOOD THAT I DIDN'T WANT TO MOVE AGAIN.
BUT I WAS WRONG. SOMEONE WAS LOOKING OUT FOR ME.
SOMEONE ALWAYS IS.

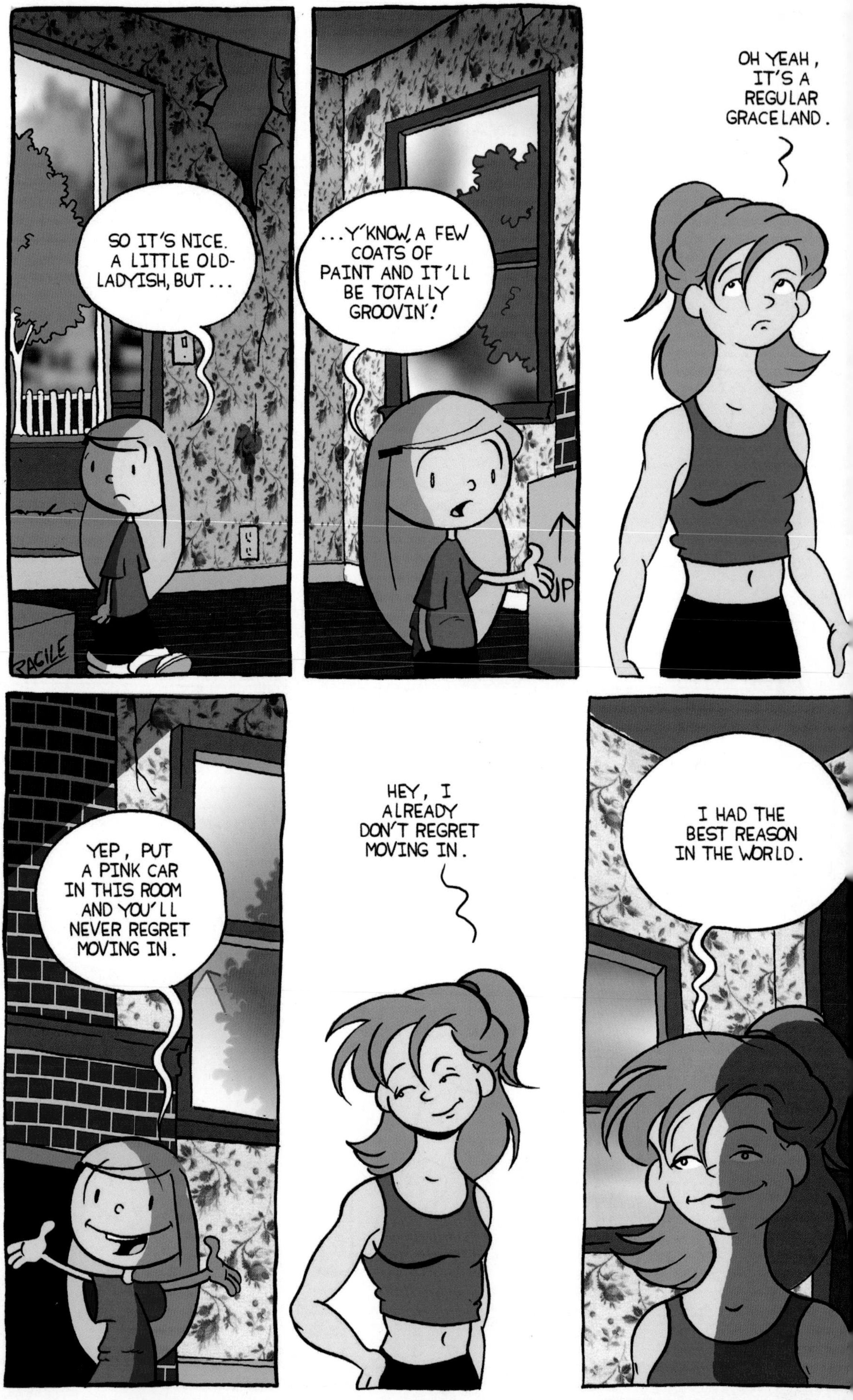
SO IT'S NICE. A LITTLE OLD-LADYISH, BUT...
...Y'KNOW, A FEW COATS OF PAINT AND IT'LL BE TOTALLY GROOVIN'!
OH YEAH, IT'S A REGULAR GRACELAND.
YEP, PUT A PINK CAR IN THIS ROOM AND YOU'LL NEVER REGRET MOVING IN.
HEY, I ALREADY DON'T REGRET MOVING IN.
I HAD THE BEST REASON IN THE WORLD.

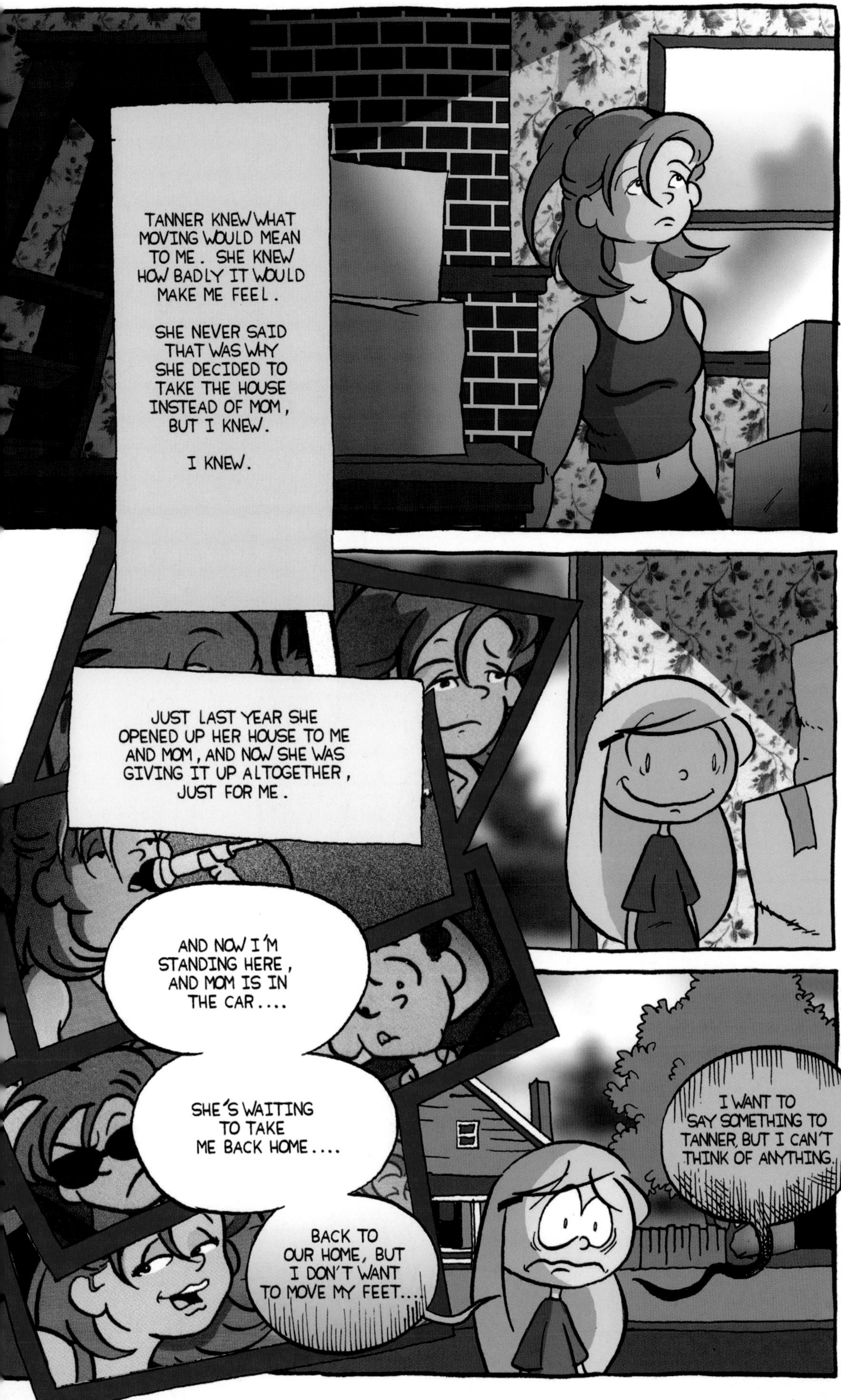
TANNER KNEW WHAT MOVING WOULD MEAN TO ME. SHE KNEW HOW BADLY IT WOULD MAKE ME FEEL.
SHE NEVER SAID THAT WAS WHY SHE DECIDED TO TAKE THE HOUSE INSTEAD OF MOM, BUT I KNEW.
I KNEW.
JUST LAST YEAR SHE OPENED UP HER HOUSE TO ME AND MOM, AND NOW SHE WAS GIVING IT UP ALTOGETHER, JUST FOR ME.
AND NOW I'M STANDING HERE, AND MOM IS IN THE CAR....
SHE'S WAITING TO TAKE ME BACK HOME....
BACK TO OUR HOME, BUT I DON'T WANT TO MOVE MY FEET...
I WANT TO SAY SOMETHING TO TANNER, BUT I CAN'T THINK OF ANYTHING.

SO I RUN BACK IN AND
I JUMP UP ON HER AND
I'M HUGGING HER AROUND
HER NECK AND I START
CRYING AND SHE STARTS
LAUGHING AND I
STILL CAN'T THINK
OF ANYTHING TO SAY.

BUT IT DOESN'T MATTER,
CUZ SUPERHEROES
NEVER NEED TO BE
THANKED ANYWAY.

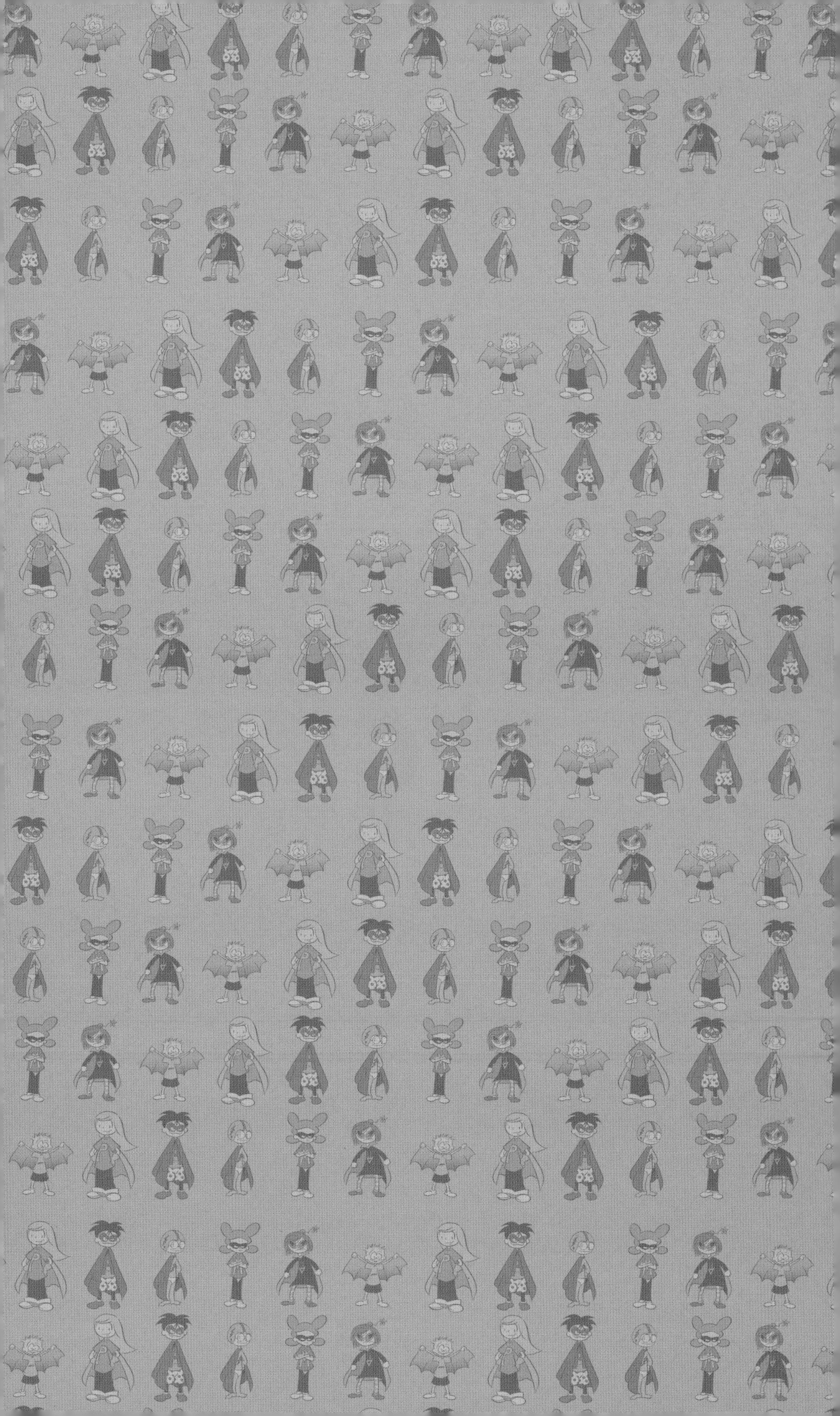